WITHDRAWN

HOT BRAZILIAN DOCS!

The night is theirs…

Brothers Marcos and Lucas escaped the *favelas* of Sao Paolo at a young age and have risen up in the world to become two top-of-their-class surgeons. Marcos and Lucas may think they can handle any curveball life throws at them, but when they come face to face with two feisty, fiery women suddenly these Brazilian docs are further out of their depth than they've ever been before!

Hold on tight and experience sizzling Brazilian nights with the hottest doctors in Latin America!

The *Hot Brazilian Docs!* duet by Tina Beckett is available now.

Marcos's story:
TO PLAY WITH FIRE

Lucas's story:
THE DANGERS OF DATING DR CARVALHO

Dear Reader

I'm sure all of you have read stories about long-lost relatives somehow finding each other after years apart. Whether that reunion takes place as a result of social media, an ad in the newspaper, or through the efforts of family and friends, that first meeting is often an emotional, heart-wrenching time. Depending on how many years—or decades—have elapsed, those people might even feel like strangers when they finally come together.

This kind of story provided the basis for Marcos's and Lucas's books, only their tale has an added twist. The brothers grew up two separate continents, one having been adopted while the other grew up in an orphanage in his home country. Now adults, with different last names, one thing binds them together: a promise they made many years earlier—one they each fulfilled in his own special way. I freely admit to shedding a tear or two as these characters struggled through some heartbreaking memories and reforged their connections to each other and their past.

Thank you for joining these strong men as they learn about love and loss, and as they work their way towards a happy ending with a couple of very special women. I hope you enjoy their journey as much as I enjoyed writing about it!

Much love!

Tina Beckett

The first story in Tina Beckett's
Hot Brazilian Docs! **duet**

TO PLAY WITH FIRE

is also available this month from
Mills & Boon® Medical Romance™

THE DANGERS OF DATING DR CARVALHO

BY
TINA BECKETT

MILLS
BOON®

Published in Great Britain 2014
by Mills & Boon, an imprint of Harlequin (UK) Limited,
Large Print edition 2014
Eton House, 18-24 Paradise Road,
Richmond, Surrey, TW9 1SR

© 2014 Tina Beckett

ISBN: 978-0-263-23899-0

Harlequin (UK) Limited's policy is to use papers that
are natural, renewable and recyclable products and made
from wood grown in sustainable forests. The logging
and manufacturing processes conform to the legal
environmental regulations of the country of origin.

Printed and bound in Great Britain
by CPI Antony Rowe, Chippenham, Wiltshire

Born to a family that was always on the move, **Tina Beckett** learned to pack a suitcase almost before she knew how to tie her shoes. Fortunately she met a man who also loved to travel, and she snapped him right up. Married for over twenty years, Tina has three wonderful children and has lived in gorgeous places such as Portugal and Brazil.

Living where English reading material is difficult to find has its drawbacks, however. Tina had to come up with creative ways to satisfy her love for romance novels, so she picked up her pen and tried writing one. After her tenth book she realised she was hooked. She was officially a writer.

A three-time Golden Heart finalist, and fluent in Portuguese, Tina now divides her time between the United States and Brazil. She loves to use exotic locales as the backdrop for many of her stories. When she's not writing you can find her either on horseback or soldering stained glass panels for her home.

Tina loves to hear from readers. You can contact her through her website or 'friend' her on Facebook.

Recent titles by Tina Beckett:

HER HARD TO RESIST HUSBAND
THE LONE WOLF'S CRAVING**
NYC ANGELS: FLIRTING WITH DANGER*
ONE NIGHT THAT CHANGED EVERYTHING
THE MAN WHO WOULDN'T MARRY
DOCTOR'S MILE-HIGH FLING
DOCTOR'S GUIDE TO DATING IN THE JUNGLE

*NYC Angels
**Men of Honour duet with Anne Fraser

These books are also available in eBook format from www.millsandboon.co.uk

DEDICATION

To those who keep their promises.

CHAPTER ONE

Lucas Carvalho was a lucky man.

At least, that was what his doctors told him. If only he could remember why.

It wasn't that he couldn't remember anything. He could. He knew his full name. That he was a plastic surgeon from California. That he'd come to Brazil for a medical conference.

But there were large swathes of empty space that he couldn't seem to fill with information. As if there'd been important data there at one time but it had been wiped clean with a single keystroke. Things like how he'd wound up with a sling around one arm and a surgical incision across the left side of his abdomen—or why he was now lying in a hospital bed without the foggiest notion as to how he got there.

And his brother—the person who'd been standing over him as he'd awoken from surgery three days ago, the person he hadn't seen in almost thirty years—had left the day before yesterday for the United States on important business.

Business that involved a woman.

Lucas's lips twisted. The last time he'd chased down a woman had been… His brain clicked through several files and discarded them.

Nope. Never happened. Never would.

At least he hoped he hadn't done anything crazy in that blank space where most of his recent memories should be.

The cute little nurse who'd come to visit him a couple of times had assured him that *he* was the one who'd talked his brother into going after that particular woman.

He struggled into a sitting position, wincing as pain sliced through his shoulder, the sling that secured his arm doing little to prevent his stitches from feeling like they were tearing free from his wound.

Not wound…wounds. Two, to be exact.

That's what the police had told him…that he'd been shot. Twice. Right outside the entrance to a nearby slum. And like his doctors, the law enforcement officials insisted he was lucky to be alive.

Today he didn't feel quite so thrilled about that fact. Actually, he didn't feel thrilled about much of anything. The aches and pains, dulled by strong doses of medication a couple of days ago, now bit into his flesh with every movement.

He eyed the IV stand to his left and noted the wheels at its base. They'd had him up and walking soon after his surgery—he remembered the same warm-eyed nurse had hovered in the background, hands twisting as he'd taken his first painful, curse-filled steps. He didn't think she was assigned to his case because she hadn't helped in any way, but he couldn't shake the feeling that she'd wanted to say something to him.

But she hadn't.

Shifting to the side of the bed where his IV bag hung, he let his legs dangle over the edge, hands gripping the mattress as he thought about his best course of action—the first being a much-needed trip to the john.

Which he could manage on his own.

He hoped.

His feet hit the floor, and the world spun for several nauseating seconds, causing him to clutch the pole beside him with a low curse.

Three days.

Surely he should be more ambulatory than this by now. The wave of dizziness passed and he stayed in place another minute or two to get his bearings. Then he leaned on the IV stand as he wheeled it toward the bathroom.

Doing the deed was a marvel in logistics co-ordination, but he somehow made it to the finish line without doing a face plant, and even washed and dried his uninjured hand afterwards.

There. He felt more independent already.

Right.

Judging from the pale face staring at him in the mirror, he might *feel* independent but he could use a big infusion of some kind of miracle drug. He jabbed his fingers through his hair, pushing it back off his forehead, not that it helped much.

Now that he was up, though, there was no way he was climbing back in that bed and staring at the dull white ceiling for hours on end. He'd done enough of that. So if walking would get him out of this place any faster, he would do just that. In fact, he'd jog if he had to.

All by himself.

He ignored the remote control dangling by its cord off the side of the bed and slogged his way toward the door, feeling like he was pushing through a huge vat of Jell-O. He refused to call for a nurse who would fuss over him like he vaguely remembered his brother doing when they'd been kids. At least until he and Marcos had been separated and grown up on two completely different continents.

His birth country had evidently missed him as much as he'd missed it, judging from the two slugs the doctors had dug out of him. His mouth twisted. Maybe he should have just stayed in the States.

Taking a deep breath and hoping he wouldn't live to regret the move, he pulled the heavy metal lever on the door and stepped into the hallway.

As a testament to how utterly fantastic his last couple of days had been, the door hit him squarely on the ass as it closed, almost sending him and his IV pole spinning to the floor.

He bit back a whole string of English cuss words that could get him into trouble, even here in Brazil, and pulled himself upright.

It's a beautiful day in the neighborhood...

With a heavy sigh of resignation he started down the long corridor in search of some answers. Or a good stiff drink. Whichever he came across first.

Nossa Senhora do céu!

Sophia Limeira's eyes nearly popped out of their sockets.

As head nurse, she should probably show a little more dignity but, *Deus*, she couldn't help but stare in awe as every female head—patients and visitors alike—turned in graceful synchronization to watch Lucas Carvalho make his way down the hall.

Long legs showed off the beautiful lithe movements of someone who knew the effect he had on those around him. Even with his left arm in a sling and dragging an IV stand along with him, he could have crooked a finger at any woman in the place and she'd have rushed toward him, snarling and snapping at anyone who dared get in her way. Even eighty-seven-year-old Marta Silva, who was parked in a wheelchair against the south wall, looked like she might slither from her seat and land in a heap at his feet.

Thankfully, Sophia was firmly anchored in her office chair—behind the desk that sat directly in Lucas's path.

It was then she noticed he wasn't making the slightest effort to hold his hospital gown closed at the back.

Maybe that was why all the women were ogling him.

It wasn't entirely his fault, as both his hands

were occupied with other things but, still, she was really, *really* glad he was facing her.

Although that was ridiculous. She was a nurse, for heaven's sake. She'd seen plenty of bare masculine butts over the last ten years.

But none of their owners had looked like Lucas.

She touched the flesh above the right side of her lip with her index finger, self-conscious all of a sudden, although she knew she didn't need to be. The scar was barely visible—the lip margins perfectly aligned. A dot of concealer on a sponge and the flaw almost blended away into nothingness.

Almost.

But Lucas was a plastic surgeon. His knowing eye could cut right through the thin layer of make-up and see the scar for what it was. A remnant from her childhood. She wondered if he ran across many cases like hers in his practice.

Probably not. He was from California, the land of beautiful bouncing breasts and perfect spray-on tans.

She gulped as his eyes met hers, then narrowed slightly, as if trying to place her.

He didn't remember her. Even when she'd slid into his room that first day and introduced herself, there'd been no hint of recognition. Even when she'd stood nearby as he'd taken his first steps.

Marcos had once said no one could forget her.

Ha! Well, someone could. And someone had.

Not that it mattered. It had been ages since she'd seen Lucas. And they'd both been children at the time.

And he'd been so very sad that first week at the orphanage. Within a month, however, they'd become inseparable—the dynamic trio, the workers had dubbed them.

Only Lucas had been one of the lucky ones who'd been adopted, leaving Marcos and her behind for ever.

Deus! He was still headed her way. And the bony hollows of the boy she'd once known were now filled in with muscle and sinew that rippled with every step he took.

Fully man. Fully dangerous.

She knew she should be on her feet, scolding him for getting out of bed and walking unassisted, but she couldn't seem to make her body obey the normal commands. Casting a quick glance around her, she saw there wasn't another nurse in sight. Just her. And Lucas's eagle-eyed gaze was fastened directly on her.

Needing to be the first one to speak for some crazy reason, she arched a brow when he reached the desk. "You do know you're putting on quite a show for the folks behind you, don't you?"

He frowned for a second then gave her a slow smile as if realizing what she meant. "Don't worry. I eventually have to go back the way I came."

Yes, he did.

Holding tight to her impassive "nurse" demeanor when all she wanted to do was keep staring, she forced a shrug. "Don't worry," she parroted. "I'm immune."

"Ah, yes, a sad byproduct of the nursing profession."

"The same can be said of plastic surgeons," she lobbed back.

See? She could be just as suave and sophisticated as he could.

"Ah, but I could never grow immune to the wonders of the female body."

Scratch that last thought. She might be able to put on a pretty good act but she could never be as sophisticated as he was. Inside, there were still remnants of the shy little orphan she'd once been. One who'd latched onto Marcos's hand the day he'd arrived at the orphanage, while shooting his

cute little brother surreptitious peeks from beneath childish lashes. She'd been bowled over by
Lucas then, and as aggravating as it might be, it
appeared she was still flustered by him now.

Tall, at six feet two—at least, according to his
chart—with dark wavy hair that hung low on his
forehead and even darker eyes, he was mesmer-
izingly beautiful. Kind of apt for someone in his
line of work, but Sophia could swear his good
looks owed nothing to plastic surgery. There were
faint crinkles radiating from the corners of his
eyes and a long line bracketed his left cheek, evidence of a slightly lopsided smile that she could
remember even from his childhood.

The times he'd smiled, that was.

Both brothers had seemed strangely grown
up, even as young children. Which made sense,
considering they'd lived in one of the notorious
favelas that dotted the landscape.

And although Lucas still spoke flawless Portuguese, an American accent threaded its way
through each and every word, sending shivers
over her each time he opened his mouth.

Or she could just be catching the flu.

Realizing she hadn't responded to his outrageous comment, she climbed to her feet, hoping the added height would snap her back to normal.

Mistake. Because her eyes only came up to his neck, where a pulse beat a steady tattoo against his skin.

Time to send him on his way. "Now that you've had your fun, do you need help getting back to your room?"

As nonchalant as he might appear, she couldn't forget he was less than a week out of major surgery to repair damage to his liver. And when she glanced higher, she spied a tell-tale glimmer of moisture across his upper lip, but he held her gaze with a steadiness that surprised her.

He shook his head, his eyes trailing down her face then pausing to retrace their path, a slight pucker appearing between his dark brows. She forced herself to remain still when he reached across the desk, his thumb brushing the area just below her right nostril and sliding to the bottom of her lip. Her heart rate shot through the roof, stomach quivering at the unexpected contact. She should be furious at his audacity, angry at how quickly he'd noticed what she'd done her best to hide, but the warmth of his skin somehow blotted out everything…except the sensation of flesh sliding against flesh.

She swallowed then answered his unspoken question. "I was born with a cleft lip. It was repaired when I was one."

"I'm sorry, I shouldn't have…" For the first time he looked uncomfortable.

Uncomfortable with what? The image of how she must have looked before her reconstructive surgery?

Surely not. But this was a man who sold beauty for a living…who knew perfection—or imperfection—the second he saw it.

Very few people ever spotted her scar. And she'd had enough attention from the male population to know that her curves tended to be the first thing a man noticed about her. Maybe that was a blessing.

But she couldn't count the number of times she'd wished a man would look into her eyes rather than stare down the front of her shirt.

Yeah? Well, here was one who had, and look what he zeroed in on.

"Don't worry about it. I'm sure in your line of work…" She let the words hang in mid-air.

His brows went up. "Why do I get the feeling

the last part of that comment would have been less than flattering."

"Not unflattering, just realistic. I'm sure your training lends itself to searching for flaws and then fixing them."

"Ah, yes. Well, if that were the case, I have two pretty big flaws right now, don't I?"

She blinked in surprise. "Really? And what would those be?" Because she couldn't see the slightest hint of any defect in the man standing in front of her. In fact, she *was* kind of looking forward to the moment when he'd turn around and walk away, just so she could get a peek at what all the other people in the wing could still see.

He lifted his bandaged arm. "Bullet holes tend to announce their presence in no uncertain terms."

Yes, they did. And that was her cue to get this man back to bed where he belonged.

Deus! That last thought carried a few more Freudian connotations than she cared to admit.

A laugh bubbled up her throat before she could stop it, and she slapped a hand over her mouth, eyes wide.

"What?" he said.

"Nothing. We just need to get you back in...in your room before you collapse."

His glance tracked to her chest, where her name-tag hung, and then back up to her face. "Sophia, right? You were in the hospital after my surgery."

The laughter dried up in a flash. "Yes."

"And when I took my first steps after the surgery."

She nodded. "I work here."

The words sounded ridiculous, even to her, but she did *not* want to explain that they'd met before. Or ask if he remembered her from when he'd been four years old. Of course he wouldn't. He'd had a brand-new life in a brand-new country. Even his last name was different now than it had been when he'd been at the orphanage.

The weird thing was that seeing him again dredged up that infantile crush she'd had on him way back when—her very first memory from her childhood days. She'd seen that beautiful face and stared at him in awe…right before she'd grabbed hold of Marcos's hand instead—too afraid to say anything to the boy standing next to him. She'd warmed up to him later but it had been a very different warmth from what she was feeling right now.

Those brown eyes touched on her scar once more and then brushed across her lips. Could he sense her thoughts? *Deus*, she hoped not. With a rough indrawn breath his gaze left her and moved to his uninjured hand, which was still hanging onto the IV pole, knuckles white as his grip tightened further. "I think you're right. I've had about all I can stand for one day. Would you mind giving me a hand?"

Sophia steadied her emotions and drew on years of training. "Sure."

Moving around the desk, she commandeered the IV stand and tucked her shoulder beneath his arm. "You ready?"

Even as he gritted out an affirmative, and they started to make their way back down the corridor, she was very aware of the warmth of his body against hers and the fact that her arm was resting across naked skin where his robe parted. Her heart shivered a couple of times then leaped into space, landing at the bottom of her abdominal cavity with a thud. It didn't quite shatter, but there was definitely a crack or two lining its tough protective surface.

Get real, Sophia. He's just one more patient in a long list of patients. He'll be gone in a matter of days or at the most a few weeks.

Maybe it was better if he never remembered

her. If she never mentioned their time together at the orphanage.

She attempted small talk as they shuffled back down the hallway. "It's really *bacana* that you and your brother found each other after all these years."

"Bacana?" Lucas stopped for a second to look down at her.

She searched around for an English word that would get across the meaning. "It's um…cool. Good."

"Yes. Very cool." The way his muscles stiffened at her words made her wonder if he really did think it was. But why wouldn't he? Marcos was a great guy. Besides, now he could get to know his home country. Get to know someone he'd once been close to.

Unlike her, who had no one. Whose parents, although still alive, had left her at an orphanage when she'd been a baby because they hadn't had the money to deal with her defect—an unfortunate reality in her country.

They'd reached out to her once, when she'd moved into her teenage years, when her government-funded surgery had been but a distant memory, but things had been strained and neither her parents nor her had particularly wanted to pick up the pieces. They'd moved to another part of Brazil by the time she'd reached adulthood, and although she still had their address, she'd never bothered to get back in touch with them. And they'd never contacted her again.

Her downed heart rolled around, reminding her of its presence. Hmm…maybe those cracks in it weren't so new after all. Maybe, like her lip, they'd healed with barely a trace. Until a hard knock—or the gentle brush of a thumb—had brought back all the reasons she needed to be on guard.

Especially with a man who'd spied what lay beneath her make-up within the space of a heartbeat but hadn't been able to see beyond it. Lucas had touched her scar back then as well—when it had been fresher and more noticeable. Before she'd learned how to cover it up with the quick flick of her make-up brush.

Surely she'd be able to do the same with her heart. By the time she was done, no one—not even the plastic surgeon by her side—would be able to see through the carefully applied layers.

And that was just the way she wanted it.

CHAPTER TWO

LUCAS HAD JUST perched on the edge of his bed when a buzzing sound came from the nurse's pocket.

"Oh, sorry. I was expecting your brother to call me this morning between rounds. He wanted to check on you."

He waved her away. "Go ahead."

His legs felt like spaghetti, despite his trash talk a few minutes ago at the nurses' station. He hated feeling helpless. Hated being at someone else's mercy.

Something about that fact tickled the back of his subconscious. A memory he couldn't quite grasp no matter how hard he tried.

Sophia pulled the phone from her pocket, her eyes still on his as she checked the readout. "It's Marcos. I'm sure he'll want to say hi."

Answering the phone, her eyes sparkled as she chatted with his brother, asking him about how things were going in the States. Something he said made her laugh. "Well, tell Maggie I send my love."

The way she said those words made a warm current flow through his chest. He hated to admit it, but being back in Brazil wasn't like he'd expected it to be. Friendships here seemed more intimate somehow, not like the superficial relationships he tended to foster. Or maybe it was because Marcos and Sophia knew each other well…maybe they'd worked together for years.

"Sure. He's right here." Sophia pressed the mouthpiece to her shoulder. "He wants to talk to you."

Lucas held out his hand, waiting as she placed the cellphone in his palm. The instrument was still warm from being in her pocket, and he hesitated before lifting it. Something about knowing she'd breathed into the receiver—had held it close to her lips, made the heat in his chest spread to his gut. It had to be the after-effects of the anesthesia and pain pills he'd had during and after his surgery. They hadn't completely cleared his system yet. He took a quick breath and held the phone close to his ear, not quite letting it touch his skin.

"Hi, Marcos. How's it going?" He spoke in English, feeling awkward talking to his brother in Portuguese. After all, he hadn't even been able to understand a simple slang term the nurse had used.

The medical conference had seemed the perfect venue to visit his home country and learn more about his culture. Unfortunately it had only served to show him how little he knew—it was just one more place he didn't belong.

His brother's amused tone brought him back to the present. "Everything's fine. I thought I'd check and see how the hospital was treating you." A female voice murmured in the background, and his brother's response came through muffled, indicating he'd turned his head to answer whoever it was.

He rolled his eyes. Surely Marcos wasn't actually in bed with his new... Searching for a word, he came up blank, as he wasn't quite sure what kind of relationship the two had. All he knew was that when he'd introduced himself to Dr. Maggie Pfeiffer at the medical conference, a glare from across the room had hit him like a fist to the jaw. He hadn't known who Marcos was at the time but he'd recognized that pointed stare. It had said *off-limits* and *mine* in no uncertain terms.

He couldn't blame his brother. Maggie was beautiful, her ready smile showing her love of life.

Not like Sophia, whose prickly attitude a few

minutes ago seemed strange, seeing as they didn't know each other. Maybe she'd had a bad day or maybe she was just that way with everyone. He glanced at her to find her busy straightening things on his bedside table, her scrubs doing nothing to detract from the generous curves beneath them.

He realized he was staring when Marcos repeated the question about the hospital.

"Everyone's been great," he said. "Thanks. The police still want to depose me in a day or two, and I should probably stick around for a couple of weeks to see if they make an arrest. So I'll take you up on your offer to stay in your apartment, if it's still okay."

"Absolutely. I told the doorman you might be coming. He has a set of keys. So does Sophia. Make yourself at home."

The thought of Sophia having a set of Marcos's house keys made him uneasy. "Thanks. I really appreciate it."

More murmurs sounded in the background, and that was definitely Marcos chuckling at something. Hand tightening on the phone, he realized he now had the thing mashed to his ear. So much for not letting it touch him any more than necessary. The fire in his gut burned just a little bit hotter when he caught a faint whiff of her scent clinging to the thing. His glance swung back to the nurse, wondering how he knew what she smelled like.

It's your sick imagination, bud.

As soon as he got back to the States, he was going to sink deep into the first willing woman he came across. It had obviously been far too long since he'd gotten any. Maybe he'd even find someone here in Brazil at one of the clubs, if he was here long enough.

"Well, I'll let you go." Lucas was suddenly anxious to get off the phone.

"Okay… Oh, wait. I forgot to ask. How does it feel to see Sophia again after all these years? It's hard for me not to still picture her as a little kid."

Little kid? That was the *last* thing he'd pictured when he'd looked at Sophia. But Marcos's words made a slight chill come over him, dousing the flames that had begun licking at places he'd rather were left alone.

"I don't follow."

There was a pause. "You don't remember her? I guess it was so long ago that—"

"Remember her from where?" The chill grew.

When he glanced to the side, he noted Sophia had turned toward him.

Before Marcos's next words came over the line, he knew he'd somehow missed something. Something big.

"She was at the orphanage with us. Stuck to our sides like glue. *O trio dinâmico.* Ring a bell?"

The dynamic trio.

Why hadn't she said anything?

"I…" Feeling like an idiot, Lucas stared at the woman in front of him, trying to see something that rang a bell. Instead, he settled for the first lame words that popped into his brain. "I was just a kid."

"Right." The disappointment surrounding that single word cut him to the quick.

How could he be expected to remember something that had happened thirty years ago? It wasn't like he'd spent his whole life in Brazil, the way Marcos had. But it did explain why Sophia had been there each step of the way during his surgery and recovery. He suddenly felt like a first-class heel.

He tried to explain. "There've been things I haven't been able to remember since the shooting. Maybe that's why."

Sophia turned away, just as Marcos said, "Don't worry about it. Could you pass the phone back to her, please?"

"Sure."

"Take care, Lucas."

"You too."

Jiggling the phone in his hand and not sure if he should just tap her on the shoulder or say her name, he settled for clearing his throat, even though the last thing he wanted to do was face her again. "He wants to talk to you."

She turned back around and gave him a cheery smile then held out her hand, her eyes skipping away from his almost immediately.

Like a man caught in a riptide and unable to pull free of its deadly grasp, he slowly handed over the phone. Then he did the unthinkable. He took a step closer and cupped her chin, his thumb strumming over the softness of her cheek as he forced her to meet his eyes. "Why didn't you say something about the orphanage?"

She took a step back, dislodging his hand. "It didn't seem important."

Not wanting to give him a chance to respond, she put the phone to her ear. "Hello?"

And proving they were indeed brothers, the first words out of Marcos's mouth were, "You didn't tell him?"

This wasn't a conversation she wanted to have in front of Lucas. Turning on her heel, she left the room. Once outside the door, she gulped down a couple of quick breaths, leaning a shoulder against a wall. With a shaky hand she brushed her hair off her forehead. "No. Why would I? Like he said, we were just kids. It's ancient history."

But the tremor in her voice said the same thing her heart did: she'd remembered *him*. Despite their ages.

What did it matter?

Exactly. She was being ridiculous. Lucas was alive—that was the only important thing. He'd be able to get on with his life as if this little interlude in Brazil had never happened. It was fine.

Her friend's voice came back through. "Well, since it's ancient history, I kind of feel funny asking you to…"

As if at a loss, he didn't finish his sentence.

"Asking me to what?"

"Check in on him every once in a while at the apartment? Make sure he's okay."

She gulped. That was so not a good idea. Lucas already made her pulse race, and he didn't even know who she was. It was one thing to act the part of his nurse at the hospital...but outside of it? "I don't know."

"Please, Soph. I know it's not fair to ask you, but you're the closest thing to family I have. You were practically a sister to us, whether he remembers it or not."

"You and I grew up together. You only remember me because we were at the orphanage longer than he was. He doesn't remember anything about his life here in Brazil."

That wasn't entirely true. She'd heard Marcos talk to Lucas after his surgery, and he'd remembered some things from his childhood. He'd remembered his brother. Remembered the promise he and Marcos had made to their father—those words were tattooed on his arm, in fact, along with his father's name. Lucas even remembered the policeman who'd found the two boys sorting through a pile of garbage at their tiny shack of a house all those years ago.

Despite all that, Lucas probably didn't recall much about his father's sudden death or what had come afterwards.

She tried again. "I'm a complete stranger to him, Marcos."

"Possibly. But you're not a stranger to me."

And there it was. He was calling up the friendship card. It wasn't like she hadn't given him enough grief over the years: Getting into trouble. Nagging. Matchmaking.

The matchmaking bit had worked out pretty well, actually, since it had given him Maggie. Still, in all the years she'd known him Marcos had never really asked anything of her. How could she say no and face herself in the mirror?

Sighing, she tipped her head against the wall and stared at the ceiling. "Fine. I'll try, but only if he lets me."

She brushed off Marcos's thanks and murmured a quick goodbye, more than ready to be done with this particular conversation. Almost as soon as she hit the "end" button, a sudden swish of air brushed her left arm, making her tense.

Her head came off the wall, and she turned to find that Lucas had silently come through the door of his room, with no warning rattle from his IV pole to alert her. She couldn't keep her gaze from tracking over him, pausing at the top of his hand, where a thin trickle of blood marred his tanned skin.

She frowned. "Where's your IV?"

That's why she hadn't heard him. He'd pulled the catheter out of his vein.

"I don't need it any more."

Right. Marcos wanted her to take care of him? Well, they were off to a great start. "That's for your doctor to decide." She motioned to the door. "I'll get you hooked back up."

He pressed the needle puncture against the fabric over his thigh, drawing her attention to the fact that he was still in his hospital gown. Still naked beneath it.

A slow breath hissed between his teeth. "I feel like I should say something here. About what Marcos said about the orphanage—"

"No need to worry about it. Like you said, we were young. You'd just had your whole life torn apart. You would have clung to the one person who was a constant in your life: Marcos."

The words made perfect sense, but they didn't take away the tiny ache that lingered inside.

"I think I've just blocked some of those memories. The day my father…when he didn't come home… Things are just a big blur. I don't remember much more than snatches of sensation here and there." He gave a lopsided smile that didn't quite reach his eyes. "I do remember the food at the orphanage leaving something to be desired. I'm still not a big fan of beans and rice."

And that should remind her, if nothing else did, that although he was Brazilian by birth, in his heart, he was just another rich man who'd left his roots far, far behind.

Her chin went up. "And I still love them."

Something touched her wrist and then slid lower, wrapping around her index finger. She glanced down in surprise to find he was no longer putting pressure on his IV site but had hooked his finger around hers. A flare of something dangerous kicked to life inside her belly.

"They're probably going to release me in a day or two. Maybe we could meet somewhere, and you could tell me what you remember from those days. Fill in some blanks. At least until Marcos gets back."

And have him discover that, unlike him, she remembered quite a bit about their time together? That while Marcos might have been his lifeline, they'd *both* been hers? "I don't think—"

"Please. I want to know."

Deus. As much as she wanted to turn her back on him and forget their paths had ever crossed again, she couldn't. Not only because of Marcos's request but because—despite the macho display as he'd swaggered toward her desk earlier—there was a hint of something beneath the knowing smile he'd given her. Something she couldn't quite put her finger on, but it was enough that she couldn't just brush off his request.

"Okay. But until the doctor releases you, you can't go around unhooking yourself from your IV. Deal?"

The smile he gave her was just as lazy as before, but this time it reached all the way up to his eyes, making her stomach do a back flip.

This was a big mistake. She felt it in her bones. But at least if she got him tethered back to his IV pole she could keep him in one spot. And she could remain just out of reach. Far enough away that he couldn't touch her again without warning, because her finger was painfully aware that he was still holding onto it. And the cheek he'd stroked a few minutes ago still tingled.

Yes, staying out of reach was a good thing. For her own peace of mind.

And if that meant keeping him at the other end

of an IV line then the man was going to find himself pumped so full of fluids that he'd inflate like a water balloon.

And that's how he'd stay. At least until she could get herself—and her out-of-whack emotions—firmly under control.

CHAPTER THREE

"YOU'LL NEED SOMEONE at home to help you for at least a week." Lucas's doctor glanced up from his chart. "No driving or lifting anything heavier than a comb, so someone will have to take you to your physical therapy sessions. Is Dr. Pinheiro back from his trip yet?"

No, Dr. Pinheiro is not back yet.

Lucas's temper flared for a second before cooling down again. He knew the standard protocol. It was just irritating to have it recited to him by another doctor. And as far as his dear brother went, who knew when he'd blow back into town. Not that he needed Marcos to run behind him and wipe his nose any more. Those days were long gone.

Lucas steadfastly refused to glance at the quiet figure waiting in the far corner of the room and tried to work through his options. If he were in the States, he could call on any number of friends, or simply ask to be moved to a rehab center for a couple of weeks. But here…

"No, he's not back, but—"

"I'll be staying with him." The soft voice made both men look up.

Lucas's jaw clenched until it became a tight ball of muscle. "There's no need."

He somehow got the words out, though he still avoided looking directly at her. He'd already racked his brain during his week of hospitalization, searching for any glimmer of memory that included the slender wraith who always seemed to be hovering nearby. But he'd come up blank, despite what Marcos had said about the three of them sticking together at the orphanage. The guilt over that ate away at him, even though Sophia acted like it didn't matter one way or the other.

Well, it mattered to him. He had very good recall when it came to women—and Sophia was not someone he would have forgotten.

Only she hadn't been a woman back then. She'd been a young girl.

"Would you rather stay at *my* apartment?"

The wry suggestion finally made his eyes light on her, and they stared at each other for a full minute. She might have been teasing but he wasn't in the mood for games right now. Especially not with the dark thoughts that careened through his head whenever he laid eyes on her. Thoughts that made him do a mental penance dance each time they arose. It had become a vicious cycle, one he'd have no hope of breaking if they were forced to shack up together.

No, it wouldn't be shacking up.

As if aware of his thoughts, Sophia's throat moved in a quick swallow. Maybe she was about to take back her offer.

Yes. Please do.

The doctor spoke up. "Well, I'll leave you two to work out the details. Sophia, if you could free him from that IV? I'm sure he'll be glad not to be dragging it behind him any more."

Something flashed through her eyes and her teeth came down on her lip before she answered, "Of course, Doctor."

Lucas couldn't hold back a small smile. She'd been none too gentle when she'd jabbed the catheter back into his vein the other day. He could have sworn she had been trying to get a wince out of him.

For not remembering her?

There it went again. He really needed to stop dwelling on this.

The doctor left the room, and he was alone with her. His smile widened just a bit. "I could always unhook myself, you know, if it makes you more comfortable. I did it once before."

"No, I'll do it." She moved to the counter with quick, precise motions, snapping on her gloves and getting a cotton ball and sticking plaster.

As soon as she was within reach, he wrapped his fingers around her wrist. "You don't have to do this, you know."

"The doctor said to undo you."

His thumb swept across her hand, grimacing when it met latex rather than the silky skin he knew lay beneath the gloves. "I'm not talking about the IV. I'm talking about you staying with me. I'm sure there are nurses I can hire. A…" He struggled to find the Portuguese equivalent of an LPN. "The kind that come to patients' homes."

Her brows went up in that indignant way he was coming to recognize. "You think I'm not qualified?"

Hell. How did he get himself into situations like this? "No, that's not it. I just know that you're busy with your job."

"I don't normally work at night. And the hospital is close to Marcos's apartment." She tugged her hand free. "Surely you can manage for a few hours here and there while I'm at work."

Why was she so insistent? They were nothing to each other, and she'd made it pretty clear she didn't want to have much to do with him. So to spend the night in the next room—at least, he figured it would be the next room. Who knew? Maybe the bedrooms were nowhere near each other. "Don't you have someone waiting for you at home?"

She sucked in a breath then released it in a slow, steady current of air. "That doesn't really have anything to do with this situation. You're Marcos's brother, and he's a special friend."

Exactly how special?

He shook his head clear of that thought. His brother had said he'd had trouble picturing Sophia as an adult so surely... Besides, Marcos and Maggie were evidently an item now. And Sophia didn't act as if she was jealous. In fact, she seemed genuinely happy for them.

With gloved fingers she took hold of his arm. "You might want to look away."

This time Lucas was the one who lifted his brows. "I think I can handle it."

"Okay." She put the cotton ball over the catheter and slid it free of his vein, then pressed on it lightly. "Hold this for a few seconds."

He blinked at her then gave the arm in the sling a little wiggle, grimacing when it hurt more than he'd expected. "Kind of hard to do that right now."

Her face turned pink. "Oh. That's right. Sorry." She kept pressure on his wrist with her thumb for a few seconds, fingers curling around his wrist. The contact lasted long enough that Lucas began to wish he'd used his chin or something else to hold onto that cotton ball as the warmth of her skin was quickly cutting through the chill of the room.

At last she eased the compression and lifted the gauze to look. "That should do it." She dropped the cotton ball into a basin then quickly peeled apart a sticking plaster and applied it over the puncture mark.

Dragging a nearby chair to the bed, she dropped into it and regarded him with serious eyes.

"What?" For the first time he wished he actually had some real clothes on, because if a certain part of him decided to go rogue, it was going to be awfully difficult to conceal it.

"The doctor was right. We need to work out the details."

"Of?" He decided to play stupid.

"How things between us are going to work."

Okay, that rogue part was already feeling the heat.

Think of something else.

Should he refuse her offer of help? Or should he suck it up and decide to make the best of a bad situation? He'd asked her to tell him about their shared past, so he could look at it as a way to kill two birds with one stone. "How many bedrooms does Marcos's apartment have?"

"Two, of course." She leaned back and crossed her legs. "Otherwise I wouldn't have offered to stay."

"Right." And she'd just made everything worse because now he was picturing a single shared bed and Sophia's lush figure sprawled across the mattress.

She fiddled with the hem of her top. "Besides, you weren't worried about the number of bedrooms a few minutes ago when you were talking about hiring a nurse."

Bingo. But then again he doubted any other nurse was going to mess with his head the way this particular one did. And he had no idea why she affected him so much. He'd love to blame it on the pain meds, but as he'd refused to take anything yesterday or today, that was impossible.

"I wasn't expecting a hired nurse to actually spend the night."

"Oh. I think that's what the doctor intended, though." She smiled at him, her brow clearing. "I've taken the rest of the day off, so whenever you're ready we can get your discharge papers signed and be on our way."

Something about that rattled around in his brain for a moment or two before he realized what he was looking for. "You were already going to offer to stay with me, weren't you, even before the doctor said anything? Why?"

"Because Marcos asked me to."

Ah, yes. His brother, the saint. Sophia would never have agreed to do it on her own, evidently.

Even though he knew his waspish reaction was childish, he couldn't help it. Lucas had often felt guilty over the years, wondering if his brother had been adopted as well. Finding out he hadn't been…that he'd spent most of his childhood in that orphanage…was hard to swallow. He had no idea why his folks hadn't taken them both, and by the time he'd been old enough to have asked, he'd rarely thought of the life he'd left behind in Brazil. And what memories he'd had weren't ones that would make him proud.

And yet he'd permanently inscribed his father's name on his arm, along with a rod of Asclepius and the words "Promises Kept" written beneath it. He did remember both he and his brother promising their father they'd become doctors—that they'd make him feel better. Of course they hadn't been able to keep the last part of that promise. Their father had died, leaving them orphans.

To take his mind off those morbid thoughts, he slid off the bed and stood. "Well, since you seem determined to stay at the apartment, I do have one rule about this whole setup."

"And what's that?" Sophia stood as well.

"I don't want any help in the bathroom. So if you could leave me to my own devices when I'm in there, I'd appreciate it."

Her eyes went wide. "Tell me you don't do drugs."

What the hell?

"Of course not. Where'd you get that idea?"

"If you don't want anyone near the bathroom while you're there…"

"Because I intend to bathe and…" he shrugged "…do whatever else I need to do all by myself. I don't need your help."

A little scoffing sound came from her lips. "You might surprise yourself and actually *ask* for my help."

That rogue part of him began stirring right on cue, forcing him to shift his stance.

She's not helping you with anything, you idiot. The doctor—and Marcos—want her there in the event you have an aneurism or something.

Which might be now, actually, because he was desperately trying to keep his mind off the tightening sensation in his groin that just wouldn't let up.

If she didn't hurry and get him some pants, he was going to embarrass both of them. "Let's just agree to play it by ear for the next couple of days. Now, if you could send me in the general direction of my clothes…"

"Oh, about that…"

She seemed flustered all of a sudden. Or maybe it was just his imagination.

"Is there a problem?"

"Yes. Kind of." She made a production of sliding the chair back against the wall. When she faced him again, her face was back to that delicious pink color he was beginning to enjoy. "You don't actually have any clothes."

CHAPTER FOUR

"What do you mean, I don't have any clothes?"

Lucas's narrowed eyes made her want to take a step back but she forced herself to hold her ground. "You were shot, remember? Twice. You were bleeding profusely when you arrived, and we had to…cut them off."

She expected him to focus in on the last part of her sentence, but instead his gaze sharpened. "*We* had to?"

Licking her lips, she tried to explain. "I don't mean we, literally. I mean the team who worked on you."

"I see."

Did he? Because he sure didn't act like it. She didn't understand why he was so upset all of a sudden. He acted like they'd done something obscene to him while he'd been lying helpless on that table. "I assure you everyone acted professionally."

"Were you there?"

"Well, no, but—"

"You weren't?" The line of his jaw relaxed so suddenly that she found her own muscles untensing as well.

"No. None of us knew who you were when you arrived." She hurried to add, "That 'us' is also figurative."

"It's okay." He gave a half-shake of his head that seemed self-deprecating, his mouth twisting into a half-smile. And just like that his mood shifted back toward that of the charmingly flippant man who'd strolled toward her desk less than a week ago. The man whose ass she'd never quite got a good look at. "But I don't think I should leave the hospital like this, do you?"

Her own lips curved. "It didn't seem to bother you before. You're lucky we didn't have any cardiac patients milling around."

Just then, the sound of some kind of commotion made its way through the heavy metal door, along with a shout. Sophia straightened, her head turning toward the noise.

"Socorro!"

The desperate cry for help grabbed her.

She threw a glance at Lucas. "Wait here."

Pulling the door open in a rush, she saw a man

standing at the nurses' station wearing a gown just like Lucas's, only he was holding something… waving it around. She couldn't tell what it was. But what she *did* see turned her blood to ice. He'd grabbed the nurse on the other side of the desk by her wrist and looked like he was physically trying to drag her over the barrier. Then Sophia caught a glint from the thing he held in his other hand. A scalpel!

Deus!

She rushed forward, yelling at one of the other patients who'd peeked out of his room, "Dial 111! Tell Security we need someone up here now."

It was lunchtime and most of the doctors had already done their rounds so there weren't a lot of people on the floor at the moment. She shouted at the crazed patient, "Let her go."

Judging by the yelp that came from the other nurse, the man squeezed even tighter. "Stay back! This one's infected. I can see it in her face."

What?

Her eyes went to Paulina, whose skin was as white as a sheet, her free hand digging at the man's fingers, trying to get him off her. Luckily the scalpel was waving aimlessly in the air, the patient didn't seem to be actively trying to cut her.

Yet. Who knew what he might do next?

This man had to be disturbed…or high. In fact, there was a long line of stitches over his right eye and in spite of the clean hospital gown he wore, his socks were filthy and crusted with blood. Had he been in a fight? Was he drunk?

She took a few more steps, circling around the man, only to hear him growl low in his throat when she ventured too close. "It's okay," she said, deciding to play along. "We know all about the infection. She's taking medication for it."

"You're lying!" A few drops of spittle flew from between his lips.

Out of the corner of her eye she spied Lucas, who'd somehow come down the hallway on silent feet and was easing toward them. One turn of the crazed man's head and he'd see him as well. Sophia didn't dare gesture for him to get back. Besides, she was damned glad to see him, even though she'd told him to stay put. And although it seemed like hours, less than a minute had passed since she'd asked the patient to call for help.

Lucas was now about twenty feet away.

Trying to maintain eye contact with the patient, she eased further to the left, glad when the man's unblinking gaze followed her movement. It reminded her of a cobra, ready to strike at the first hint of weakness.

"I'm not lying," she murmured in as soothing a voice as she could manage. "Her hair has light streaks of color in it. It means the treatments are working."

Are you insane, Sophia? What are you trying to do?

Keep him busy. Until someone could get to them. Anything to stop that scalpel from slicing through the air and hurting Paulina.

The patient's lips thinned as his feverish gaze tripped from her to Paulina and then back again. The fingers holding the deadly weapon trembled for a second or two. "I don't see anything."

"Because you're not a doctor. You're not trained to."

Just then, Lucas succeeded in covering the last few feet that separated them and grabbed the man's knife hand. An enormous roar came up from the patient's chest. He released Paulina and pivoted with lightning speed toward Lucas. Sophia lunged forward and caught the guy's other hand to keep him from twisting the rest of the way round. The man was as strong as an ox. He threw her backwards, sending her skidding across the floor, where she flailed as she tried to maintain her balance—only to fail miserably and land on her butt.

She scrambled back up just as the sound of tinkling metal hit her ears, along with Lucas's grunt of pain when the man's fingers closed around a fistful of his hair and hung on. Before she could run toward them again, two men in uniforms stepped out of the elevator, took one look at the scene and charged, each man grabbing a gowned figure and wrestling them apart.

"Dammit! Let me go!"

The oath came from Lucas, who was now pinned securely in front of one of the guards, one elbow locked behind him, while the injured arm dangled awkwardly, the sling bunched along his forearm. Amazingly, the troublemaker had gone totally limp once subdued, moaning as if mortally wounded. He looked like the victim, rather than the guilty party.

As she put a hand to her throat and struggled to catch her breath, one of the guards glanced expectantly at her. "Which one did you call us about?"

"The one on the left."

Poor Lucas looked like he'd been through the wringer. His hair stood straight up where the other man had grabbed it and his gown had twisted sideways, revealing quite a bit of one taut thigh.

Releasing him, the guard said, "What happened?"

"That man attacked Paulina, yelling about some kind of infection."

Just then a woman exited a second elevator and rushed toward them, followed by one of the emergency room doctors.

"Please don't hurt him. I'm his sister," she said. "He's schizophrenic. I didn't realize he was off his meds until this morning when I found him covered in blood, saying someone was after him. I lost track of him in the emergency room."

The doctor nodded. "He wasn't particularly agitated when he arrived. I stepped out to call his psychiatrist, who's on his way. It'll take him about ten minutes to get here."

His sister spoke up. "I'm so sorry about all of this. My mother called and I left the room for just a second to talk to her." She glanced at Lucas and then evidently spied the scalpel on the floor. "Oh, no. Did he hurt someone?"

"No, we stopped him in time," Sophia said. The woman seemed so genuinely upset that she didn't have the heart to tell her just how serious the situation had been. And from the look of the man now, you'd never guess he'd just gone on a rampage. She could understand why they'd let their guard down.

Besides, even with all the precautions in the world, you couldn't always stop bad things from happening. She knew that for a fact. Look at Marcos and Lucas. Or even her own childhood, for that matter.

The doctor turned to the guard who'd been holding Lucas. "Could you accompany us back to the emergency wing? I'd appreciate it."

Within minutes they'd bundled the patient, whose name was evidently Ronaldo, into a wheelchair and got back into the elevator, his sister holding his hand.

Sophia sent Paulina a shaky smile. "Are you okay?"

The nurse chuckled and pressed a hand to her chest. "Other than wondering if he was going to carve out my heart and eat it, yes. Thank you for coming when you did." Her gaze went to Lucas, who leaned against the counter. "And thank you for wrestling that scalpel away from him."

Sophia realized Lucas wasn't just leaning against the nurses' station, he was propped against it as if he'd fall to the floor if he let go. "Hey. Are you hurt?"

"You mean besides my pride?"

His pride. What did that have to do with anything?

"You made him let go of the knife."

"And if those guards hadn't gotten here when they had, that's about all I would have done."

Shock whistled through her. He acted like he'd just let the opposing team score the winning goal of the season.

She moved over to him and laid a hand on his arm. "What are you talking about? You disarmed him, Lucas. You saw how he threw me across the room like a toy. If you hadn't stepped in to help, who knows what damage he could have caused?" She frowned. "Speaking of damage, how are your stitches?"

"They're not happy, but they're still there. I'll be glad when the damned things come out."

Paulina wheeled an office chair around the desk and put it behind him. "Sit, before you fall down."

"I'm fine." Despite his words, he carefully lowered himself into the chair. Was he really okay? Or just saying that for her and Paulina's benefit?

"How about your side? Did he get you?"

"No. Believe me, I was keeping everything of value as far out of the reach of that scalpel as I could."

Paulina giggled at the words, although it took Sophia a second or two to get his meaning. Then her face heated in a rush, and her glance instinctively dropped to his lap. "Oh."

"Yeah. As it was, no harm done." He dragged a hand through his hair, pausing to rub the area of his scalp where the patient had pulled his hair. "I'll give you this, Nurse Limeira, you sure do run an exciting ward here."

She laughed. "All in a day's work, Dr. Carvalho."

He sighed and leaned back in the chair, closing his eyes for a second or two.

Hmm, the man really did look a bit shaky. Maybe it was time to get him out of there. "Are you still feeling well enough to be discharged today? Or do you want to stick around for one more night?"

"And risk another scene like that one?" He shook his head. "I think I'm more than ready to leave. A nice—*quiet*—apartment is sounding better and better."

She glanced at Paulina, who seemed positively starstruck by Lucas, even going as far as to twirl a strand of her bleached-blonde hair around her index finger as she watched him.

Even injured, he had the same effect on other women that he'd had on her when she'd been little. A tiny part of her wondered if she was the only one he'd forgotten. Maybe he didn't remember any woman he'd had contact with. He was handsome enough that he could have his pick—just look at Paulina. And maybe he did just that. Maybe he went through them so fast that none of them made a lasting impression.

Her mood took a sudden nosedive. She needed to remember her earlier admonition to steer clear of him as much as possible. Not that it was going to be possible as she'd volunteered to sleep over. If it weren't for her longstanding friendship with Marcos, she wouldn't have offered in the first place. But she had, and she felt obligated to go through with it.

Well, just because she had to sleep *near* him, it didn't mean she was going to sleep *with* him.

She blinked. Why had that thought even come up?

Maybe because she'd gotten a good glimpse of rock-hard thighs and a nice tight tushie during the struggle with Ronaldo.

Yep, visions of sponge baths were now dancing through her head.

Well, there'd be none of that. Not here. Not at Marcos's apartment. She was simply there to make sure the man didn't fall and suffer a concussion.

Although if he didn't wipe that knowing smirk off his face, a concussion wasn't out of the realm of possibilities. And she'd be the one inflicting it.

She stepped in front of Paulina in an effort to snap the woman back to reality. "Well, I guess that's settled. Before we have any more mishaps, maybe we should find you something to wear and get you out of here."

CHAPTER FIVE

AT LEAST HE didn't have to wear his brother's clothes.

Lucas knew it was a strange thing to be thankful for, but he was borrowing his brother's apartment, sleeping in his brother's bed, and making use of his brother's friend.

No. She was *their* friend. At least, from what Marcos had told him.

Damn, if only he could remember.

Right now, Sophia was brewing coffee in his brother's kitchen as if she'd done it a million times. That thought made him uneasy and he wasn't sure why.

He should be grateful for all she was doing for him. And he was. After all, she'd gone to his hotel and arranged for his things to be taken to Marcos's place. And he hadn't had to watch her actually carry his stuff into the building while he'd trailed along behind.

Unlike her own suitcase. Which he'd been painfully aware he couldn't offer to carry. It made him feel useless, something he wasn't used to.

Perched on his brother's couch, the scent of coffee hit his nose, and he breathed deeply as he surveyed his surroundings. Modern furnishings, almost painfully so, were strategically placed, from the black leather sofa and swivel recliner to the low black cabinet where a flatscreen television sat at eye level. A photo to the left of the set caught his attention.

Struggling to his feet while trying to ignore the fierce burning in his shoulder—a direct result of the scuffle at the hospital—he moved toward the picture.

"Do you want *café com leite*? Or do you take your coffee black?" Sophia's voice came from behind him, distracting him for a second, and when he turned his head he found her peeking around the corner, a few locks of sleek black hair sliding over one bare shoulder as she leaned to the side. She flipped the strands back with a quick shake of her head, leaving a long line of tanned skin that seemed to call out to him.

Damn. He knew she had a shirt on, he'd seen it—some kind of fluttery green thing that wrapped around her just above the swell of her breasts.

There were no straps, though, so right now all he could think about was how she'd look if she stood in that exact pose *without* the shirt. And, boy, could his imagination drum up a pretty good set of possibilities.

"Lucas?" she said. "What do you want in your coffee?"

Besides you?

He shook himself back to reality. "Just a couple of drops of sweetener, if Marcos has any." Artificial sweetener in Brazil came in plastic bottles, he'd found, although some of the higher-end coffee shops carried packets of the stuff, along with sugar.

"Okay, I'll be out in a minute." A quick smile accompanied the words, and she popped back into the kitchen.

Lucas braced a hand on the television stand, swearing softly. He probably should have suggested that he hole up in his hotel room for another couple of weeks. *Had* suggested it, in fact, once his discharge papers had been written up, but Sophia had held him to his promise of letting her help—compliments of his brother. Again. The tattoo on his arm was a constant reminder that he kept his word when at all possible. He hadn't been able to keep much of anything else in his life—not even his real last name—so it was the one thing he'd felt he had control over.

So he was stuck with her. For now.

Brazilian women tended to dress to accentuate their curves, and Sophia was no exception. There was no way he was going to tell her to change for his benefit. But he also hadn't expected to be knocked for a loop by seeing her out of her customary scrubs either.

The slim white jeans she wore hugged her body, cupping her curves in all the right places. Then there was that blouse, the deep green fabric snug on top before floating down around her hips, the silky fabric molding to her form whenever she moved. It was almost long enough to be a dress—a teeny-tiny one. And those heels...

Whew.

Despite the sexy clothes, there was a youthful innocence to Sophia, although he couldn't quite put his finger on why she gave off that vibe. It wasn't that she was a child—he shifted his aching shoulder as he turned back toward the framed photo on the television table—far from it. But there was a certain *joie de vivre* that clung to her as tightly as her narrow slacks. Strange that she would give off that kind of glow, despite growing up in a bare bones orphanage. Or after what she must have gone through with her facial surgery.

The narrow scar on her lip had made something contract inside him. Maybe because he spent almost all of his vacation time treating children in developing countries with just that type of deformity. The fact that Sophia bore the telltale mark of a surgeon's tools made his heart cramp.

There was something about the scar that struck a chord deep inside him. And touching it as she'd stood behind the desk at the nurses' station had triggered a visceral reaction that had been both foreign and familiar. Those two sensations had warred within him for several seconds. Had he remembered the scar from their time together at the orphanage?

Possibly.

It wasn't a real memory, per se, more a remembered emotion. Curiosity, maybe? It hadn't been disgust. Far from it. But it seemed to mesh with his reasons for choosing pediatric reconstructive surgeries over the more lucrative types.

Pulling his focus back to the picture, he picked it up. Two adults and two children were grouped around a rickety handcart. The image was real.

Not one of those staged, stick-your-head-through-the-cardboard-figure kind of thing he saw from time to time. He narrowed his eyes and tried to see the details past the sepia tones and the midline crack where the picture had evidently been folded at one time. A man stood at the metal bar across the front of the contraption and held the cart level, while a woman and baby perched on the flat bed, and the older child with a grubby T-shirt and worn flip-flops stood with his hands on his hips, legs braced apart.

Lucas swallowed. It was them—his birth family—he knew it even without being told. His mom held him close in a protective gesture, while his brother dared the world to mess with any of them.

His father already looked broken down, even back then. Staring at the picture, he tried to sense some kind of emotional connection with the figures, but felt only a vague sense of shame, which was probably left over from days gone by. His brother's feet were the only thing that elicited a strong reaction in him. He had shoes on, while his own feet were bare. He did remember snatches of arguments he and his brother had had—with Marcos constantly railing at him for not wearing shoes in the yard.

He still preferred his feet bare, not that he got much of a chance any more with his busy lifestyle.

A soft click sounded behind him and then Sophia's voice came again. "That's you and Marcos with your parents."

The fact that Sophia didn't expect him to know what he was looking at sent another wave of shame washing over him. His adoptive parents had said they'd chosen him because the day they'd visited he'd been curled in a corner, sucking his thumb. He'd been skin and bones, and had seemed hopeless, they'd said…so much so that it had frightened them. They'd never thought about having kids of their own—although they'd worked with several children's charities—until they'd seen him.

They'd given him opportunities that few kids in his situation would have ever dreamed of having. And that just compounded his guilt, even though Marcos and Sophia seemed to be doing just fine, judging by the high-end furniture in his brother's apartment. In fact, the picture was the only shabby-looking thing in sight.

He set the frame back in its spot and turned toward her. "I'll have to ask Marcos to make a copy for me."

"Do you remember them at all?"

He hesitated. "I think I remember my father and Marcos, but not my birth mother."

"She died when you were still a baby." She reached back and bunched her long hair in her hand, then twisted it and tied it somehow so that it stayed up off her neck. "Your parents loved you very much, from what Marcos says. Your adoptive family must have as well."

"They did. I guess I was lucky."

He'd called them, in fact, after the shooting. They'd been worried sick, had wanted to come down immediately, but he'd assured them he was fine and would be back in the States soon.

Sophia turned away and walked to the glossy coffee table. "I brought the bottle of sweetener and a spoon. I wasn't sure how much you wanted."

Her words were tight, and he got the feeling he'd said something wrong. Was she upset because he'd been adopted and she hadn't? Surely not. He'd had no choice in the matter. Looking back, though, he could certainly see how hard it must've been for Marcos to be the one left behind. But he was glad his brother had been there for Sophia.

"Thank you for the coffee." Following her, he noted one of the clear glass mugs was filled almost to the brim, while the other was only half-full. He found out why when Sophia tipped a white pitcher of milk into the one with less coffee. He smiled. "When you say *café com leite*, you mean it."

"Brazilian coffee is stronger than what you serve in the States, at least from what I've heard."

A barista at a local coffee shop had jokingly referred to American coffee as "*água suja*" or dirty water. And compared to the dark, full brew that most Brazilians preferred, he could see why.

Sophia settled onto the sofa and took a sip of her drink with a sigh.

You could tell the apartment belonged to a bachelor by the lack of seating options. It was either sit beside her or try to perch on the low-slung easy chair to the right of it. And his side still bothered him enough that he chose the sofa over his sense of self-preservation. So once he'd doctored his coffee, he sat next to her, waiting for the surgical sites to settle down before he took his first slug.

The dark liquid was smooth, with a slightly bitter aftertaste that lingered on his palate the way good coffee should. He closed his eyes and let the scent and taste fill his senses. "I'm glad I didn't drink the hospital's coffee before I left. This was worth the wait."

She smiled at him and bumped his uninjured shoulder with hers before kicking off her heels and curling deeper into the sofa. "I'm glad you like it. And thanks again for your help with that patient. I was worried you'd ripped your stitches."

"Does that kind of thing happen often?"

"No more than at any other hospital, I suppose. You've never had a patient go berserk on you?"

"My patients are generally a lot smaller than that one."

Her lips twisted. "That's right, most of yours are probably women who are looking for a tune-up."

"Actually, no. I work with children. I'm a pediatric plastic surgeon. I deal with…" He swallowed at what he'd been about to say and changed the words slightly. "Facial reconstructive surgery, usually after a traumatic injury."

Her finger went to her lip, the way it had a number of other times. Surely she wasn't self-conscious about it. No one but a surgeon who dealt with cleft lips on a regular basis would be aware of her scar. "Why do you do that?"

She didn't ask what he meant. "Maybe because you noticed it right away."

"I didn't. Only after you touched it that first day." He wasn't about to tell her he hadn't been looking at her lip when he'd seen her at the desk. Or that there'd been something about her that had drawn him toward her, as it did even now.

He'd thought it had been because he'd recognized her from her earlier visits, but who knew? His head had still been pretty foggy about the shooting and what had happened afterwards. Maybe he could tackle that. Get her talking so he could keep his mind off the fact that he was seated beside a beautiful woman—all alone in his brother's house. And that he couldn't seem to stop staring at her lips—not because of her scar but because they were pink and inviting and…

And he had to put a stop to this right now.

"Did the police tell you anything else about what happened?"

She shook her head. "Marcos said you were standing in front of the *favela* where you both lived as kids. The police were involved in a drug raid, and a couple of the dealers' shots hit you as they tried to evade capture."

He should remember something more about that time—like how he'd even known where he'd once lived—but it was still a blank for the most part.

"That's what the police told me as well. I just can't remember."

"It happened fast, from what I understand. Didn't the doctor say your memories should come back after a while? You banged your head pretty hard on the pavement when you went down. Unfortunately the taxi driver took off once he heard the shots, so the police had to step in. Maybe they'll find the driver and you can ask him how you ended up there." She shifted on the couch so she faced him.

"Maybe." He took another sip of coffee, trying to use the strong fragrance to blot out the more subtle scents of vanilla and flowers that drifted his way whenever she moved.

Perfume or body wash?

Perfume. It was the safer option as he really didn't want to picture her hands sliding in long soapy strokes over her body.

Hell! He'd just pictured it anyway.

"At least something good came of it," she said, her hand wandering from her knee to her ankle and curling around it. "You found your brother."

There was a hint of shadow in her tone, and Lucas wished to God he could remember her. Wished he'd been around to watch her grow into the gorgeous woman she was today. Then maybe he wouldn't be so floored every time those expressive brown eyes met his. Like right now.

"There is that." He set his coffee on the table. "So you didn't know I was a pediatric plastic surgeon?"

"Nope." She laughed. "I thought you spent your days looking at…" She let go of her ankle and waved a hand in a kind of winding motion over her chest.

Yeah, well, it seemed like he'd spent an inordinate amount of time over the last couple of days looking at just that area. And her reminding him of that fact wasn't helping an increasingly uncomfortable situation that was beginning to arise.

Fast.

"Ah…no. That never appealed to me at all." His vision shrank to a pinpoint when he realized how that sounded. "Not that I'm opposed to those who might want to…I mean, I like them and all."

Her brows lifted and she laughed. "Maybe you should quit while you're ahead."

"Maybe I should." His mouth curved as well.

They smiled at each other for a second or two then she licked her lips, drawing his attention back to them once again. "You seemed to have made a fan of Paulina this afternoon."

"Paulina?"

"The nurse who helped you sit down."

"Ah." The way she'd said it bothered him, for some reason. "I didn't make a fan of you, I take it."

"You're Marcos's brother. I don't need to be your fan."

Perfect. Just what he needed, a reminder that she was only here because of his brother, not because she found him the slightest bit attractive.

His masculinity took another hit. First, he was still as weak as a kitten, having had to be carted out of the hospital in a damned wheelchair. Then he'd been unable to even help Sophia carry her things into the building when they'd arrived. She'd had to prop him up with one arm while lugging her purse and overnight case with the other.

And now this.

"So what would it take to make you a fan, Sophia?"

"I don't know what you mean."

He tilted his head and studied her. "You don't like me very much, do you?"

"Of course I do. I'm here, aren't I?" Was that genuine surprise in her voice?

"But you're only here because of Marcos."

"I… I…" She paused as if unsure of what to say. Then she set down her coffee and reached over to touch his hand. "I'd have probably offered to help, even if he hadn't asked."

He curved his fingers around hers before she could withdraw. "Would you?"

Why was it so important to him that she wanted to be here? Maybe because this country—his homeland—made him feel like a stranger. In fact, he'd heard Sophia use that very word when she'd talked to his brother.

Her eyes held his, and she made no effort to tug her hand free. "I think so."

"So would you call yourself a fan?"

"Would you call *yourself* one?"

His fingers tightened at the faint challenge he heard in her voice. "Definitely. I think you have a lot of fans, though. My brother being one of them."

"I think you have quite a few yourself. Especially after strolling down the hallway and leaving very little to the imagination. Are you always so uninhibited?"

"Uninhibited?" He cocked a brow. "It depends on the situation."

Sophia's lips parted, giving him a glimpse of straight white teeth, and she hesitated as if trying to figure out how to respond. "You were feeling uninhibited at the hospital?"

The atmosphere in the room became thick, heating quickly. "Hmm. Maybe you have that effect on me."

"I doubt that."

"You underestimate yourself, Sophia." He released her hand and brushed a loose strand of hair back over her shoulder, his palm grazing her bare skin. It was just as silky soft as he'd imagined, and her rough intake of breath at his touch made his insides ignite. "In fact, I feel like doing something a little crazy right now. Something wild and uninhibited."

He went on, "I remember you called Security on the last guy who did something like that."

"Does what you want to do involve a scalpel?"

"No. No scalpels. But it does involve lips. Yours and mine." He upped the ante a notch, letting his fingers slide along her jaw until he cupped her chin and looked deep into her eyes. "So are you going to call Security on me, Sophia? Or can I kiss you?"

She shook her head.

He smiled. "Does that mean you're not going to scream for help? Or are you saying no to me kissing you?"

There was silence for several tense seconds, and he thought at first she was going to pull away. Then she took a deep breath.

"I won't call Security," she whispered.

"Oh, honey," he said as tiny clusters of heat burst into flame throughout his body. "I was so hoping that's what you'd say."

CHAPTER SIX

HE'D GIVEN HER plenty of warning, but nothing could have prepared her for this.

The second Lucas's lips closed over hers, her heart stumbled into a rhythm so chaotic she could swear she was going into V-tach. Any second now a monitor would start sounding an alarm and everyone would come running.

Only there was no one else here. Just her…and Lucas. And this exquisite, soul-shattering kiss. One that was nothing more than the barest touching of lips but it was more than she'd ever imagined a kiss could be.

More than it ever had been. With anyone.

His fingers sifted into her hair, the messy knot soon giving way and sending everything cascading down her back as he held her in place. But if he was worried about her moving away, he needn't be. Sophia had no intention of going anywhere.

Not yet.

Maybe not ever.

Her hands went to his shoulders and curled over them for several seconds, unsure how far he planned to take this. Testing the waters, she slid them further up until she reached his nape, then went on past, until her arms were around his neck.

He made a sound, halfway between a groan and a growl, and Sophia started to pull back in a hurry, thinking she was hurting him, only to have his fingers tighten in her hair. His good arm suddenly snaked around her waist and hauled her closer.

Oh!

Thigh to thigh, torsos twisted towards each other, Lucas finally opened his mouth. Really opened it and swept her away on a wave of longing so strong she had trouble breathing. Or that could just be the way her body was contorted.

He pulled back, lips trailing slowly towards her ear, sending a shiver over her that turned to a shudder when he whispered, "Kiss me back, Sophia."

What? She thought she had been.

No, that wasn't really true. She'd been wallowing in the heady reality that what she'd thought was an unreachable daydream wasn't so far out of the realm of possibility after all.

He *was* attracted to her. Even if he couldn't remember who she was.

Maybe it was better that way. Because the last thing she wanted right now was for him to treat her like a child.

When his mouth landed back on hers, her thoughts were buried beneath the sudden hot pressure of his lips as he urged her to keep up with him—to give back some of what she was receiving. So she parted her own lips and buried her fingers in the thick hair at the back of his head.

It wasn't long before his tongue found hers and slid along it, edging deeper and deeper until he filled her completely. A moan worked its way up from the lowest regions of her abdomen and came out before she could stop it. Not that she wanted to.

No. She wanted this. All of it. Wanted more.

Her eyes sealed shut, trying to lock out everything but the feel of him inside her. All around her. His scent, his heat.

And, God, he was only kissing her. What would happen if they actually…?

She'd wind up on life support probably.

Lucas shifted slightly, and her eyes blinked open as he drew back with a soft curse.

"What is it?" she murmured.

"My damn side."

She pulled away. "Oh, I'm sorry."

"No, stop. Don't go anywhere." He touched one of her legs. "Here, climb on top of me so I don't have to twist to reach you."

"Excuse me?"

He grinned, a flash of white teeth. "Ready to call for that rescue team now?"

She licked her lips. Climb on top of him. Like how? Surely he didn't mean for her to lie on him. If his side hurt now, she could only imagine what it would be like if she put any pressure on it. "I'm not sure—"

Leaning back on the sofa, he took hold of her hands then his fingers slid up her arms. "Straddle me. I promise I won't go any further than a kiss."

She gulped. Maybe that life-support idea wasn't so far-fetched after all.

As if he could read her thoughts, he continued, "Just sit on my knees. I'll let you keep as much distance between us as you want. But I'm not quite ready to let you go yet. Unless you want me to."

No. She didn't.

Sophia knew she was going to sorely regret this as soon as her libido had a chance to cool down, but she wasn't ready to stop yet either. Uncurling her legs and rising to her knees, she swung one leg over his thighs and started to lower herself, only to have his hands tighten on her upper arms. She glanced down to find his smoldering eyes locked on her face. "Slowly. Let me imagine."

Deus. She knew exactly what he was imagining, and her face flamed with a heat that threatened to consume her. But she did as he asked and inched her way down, until the backs of her thighs grazed his legs. She allowed her weight to settle, realizing that because of the way his hips were slouched forward, she wasn't exactly sitting on his knees. But then again she was at least six inches away from any dangerous areas. And she didn't mean his injured side.

Her hands went to the back of the sofa to brace herself, and she leaned forward to kiss him again. His palms cupped her face before she could get there, his thumb traveling in a slow arc down her scar. "You're beautiful, you know. If anything, this just adds to it."

She'd never had anyone talk so openly about her lip—an area of her body she was self-conscious about. And yet Lucas hadn't hesitated either time. He'd gone right to the spot most people tried to ignore—or maybe they really didn't notice.

Something about the way he touched it wove a silky web of desire that slowly tightened around her. "Kiss me," she said, handing his own words back to him.

Pupils widened as his thumb continued to stroke over her skin with velvety passes. "I'm right here, honey."

Whether it was because of his injuries or because he was throwing down a challenge to see if she would accept it, she arched her brows and allowed herself to slide a few inches forward on his legs.

Big mistake, because the friction just made things inside her narrow their focus, a dangerous melting beginning to take place.

"Not fair, Sophia."

He wasn't kidding. Her body was saying pretty much the same thing.

Trying to hold onto her new-found bravado, she murmured, "Very fair."

What the hell was she doing? She was straddling a man she barely knew. A couple more wiggles and she'd be into lap-dance territory.

He chuckled. "I guess it is." Using the hands that were still on her face, he drew her towards him until there was only an inch of space between them. "You, young lady, are a very dangerous woman. You're also a very, very lucky one at the moment."

She could agree on the lucky part. *Now do it!*

Instead of kissing her, however, he curled an arm around her back and settled her against his good shoulder, his hand sliding up and down her spine in a slow, soothing cadence that did anything but calm her. She blinked in confusion as his breath whispered past her ear and stirred strands of her hair.

There was still some space between their bottom halves, and she was tempted to move forward again just to see what was going on. Then the hand at her back hesitated, before moving again. Slower this time. It paused again, then took longer to start back up.

When the sound of his breathing changed—deepened—she knew the awful truth even before his palm gave one last downward pass and went completely still.

The man had fallen asleep.

The smell of bacon made his nose twitch.

He opened his eyes to find he was still on the sofa, but lying on his back, shoes off, a light blan-

ket pulled over him. And the firm, luscious bottom that he remembered resting on his thighs was
nowhere to be found.

He'd conked out? Unbelievable.

He'd been in the middle of the hottest damn kiss
of his life, everything had seemed to be up and
working like it should, and he'd just passed out in
the middle of it. He'd been planning on keeping
his promise of just kissing her, but he'd hoped to
enjoy it a little bit longer. In fact, that was why
he'd *stopped* kissing her. He'd needed to give himself a moment or two of downtime to combat the
way his senses had gone haywire as her butt had
slid across his legs. That downtime had turned
into hours, if the light pouring through the sliding glass door to his left was anything to go by.

He cranked himself upright with a groan as tight
muscles protested the movement.

Hell. He'd probably never get the chance to take
up where they'd left off. It was surprising that Sophia hadn't just left him sitting upright in a pool
of his own drool. Instead, there was a pillow with
a light blue pillowcase where his head had just
been. She'd evidently climbed off him and, ever
the dutiful nurse, had made sure he was taken
care of before she went to bed.

He blinked. Well at least he remembered what had happened last night. Mostly. Up until the part where his eyelids had come together and sealed shut. He remembered his thumb brushing across Sophia's scar repeatedly, the act once again strangely familiar. Comforting in a weird kind of way.

Yes, it was weird. And she probably didn't appreciate him drawing her attention to it over and over. It was intrusive and rude.

His already foul mood headed further south.

He shook himself out of his thoughts just as she peeked around the corner, the sensation of *déjà vu* growing until he remembered she'd done the same thing yesterday.

"Oh, good," she said. "You're awake. Do you need any help?"

He scrubbed a hand through his hair. "Hell, I'm sorry about last night. I don't know what I was thinking—"

A wooden spoon appeared around the corner, waving off his words. "You've just gotten out of the hospital. I had no business getting on your... I had no business doing any of that. I hope you'll forgive me."

Forgive her? She was acting like she'd breached some kind of professional barrier and was struggling to get back behind it.

"You're not my nurse, Sophia."

"I'm responsible for you." Even from his perch he thought he spied a glimmer of guilt in her brown eyes.

"No. You're here to make sure I don't fall and crack my head wide open."

"Exactly."

Said as if that settled everything. It didn't. It settled nothing, and a burning in his gut was now rivaling the growing pressure in his bladder. So he hauled himself up and off the sofa, ignoring the sharp pull in his side as he did so. It took Sophia's soft gasp for him to realize—far too late—that his slacks were undone, his fly stationed at the lowermost part of its track.

He looked down, his brain struggling to process the consequences of her not bringing any briefs to the hospital when she'd brought his clothes: he was now standing here in front of her…in all his questionable morning glory.

Damn. Maybe his memory of the events surrounding that kiss weren't as clear as he'd thought. But surely he'd have remembered if they'd…

He quickly zipped himself back in then his glance came up, eyes narrowing. "What exactly did we do last night?"

CHAPTER SEVEN

"WE DIDN'T DO anything!"

Sophia's face sizzled like the bacon she could hear in the background as she tried to look anywhere but below Lucas's waist.

Several large pops, followed by angry hissing and sputtering came from behind her, and she ducked back into the kitchen, more than glad to scoot away from the memory of his bare...

Okay, he hadn't exactly been sticking out of his pants when she'd undone him last night.

Rescuing the strips of bacon before they burned to a crisp, she laid them out on a paper towel as she tried to get the image of what she'd just witnessed out of her mind. She failed miserably. The shocked look in his eyes. The alarmed *zzzzip* as he'd yanked the tab of his fly back up.

She'd been trying to do him a favor last night, not wanting the tight waistband to damage the stitches in his side as he slept. She'd forgotten he didn't have on underwear, but then again...

she hadn't peeled his pants apart to look. She'd just covered him up with a blanket and that had been that.

It certainly had. Because he'd *fallen asleep*!

It still stung that not only was she not memorable as a person, she wasn't even interesting enough as a potential lover to hold his attention…during a kiss that *he* had initiated. Okay, that wasn't fair, he had still been weak from the trauma of the gunshots followed by blood loss and then surgery. Of course he'd been tired.

You'd have done the same thing, Sophia.

She'd just about convinced herself of that when he appeared in the kitchen doorway a few minutes later, his hair damp from an apparent shower and dressed in fresh clothes. Firmly zipped, she noticed. The stiff way he held his left arm as he leaned against the doorframe said that whatever he'd done in the bathroom had cost him dearly.

"You should have waited for me to help you. That's why the doctor asked me to stay, remember?"

"I think you've helped quite enough already." His mouth tightened slightly. "I'm still waiting for what promises to be a very interesting explanation."

"No explanation needed. You fell asleep, and I didn't want to undress you all the way, so I settled for opening…"

Okay, well, that hadn't come out exactly right.

One brow went up. "I'm regretting nodding off more and more."

Despite the tension still radiating off him, the words came out with a trace of lazy humor. The last thing Sophia wanted, however, was for him to think she'd ogled him in his sleep. Or worse.

"I was only thinking about the stitches on your abdomen."

"That's not what I was thinking about at all. Especially last night."

Right. She could tell. Which was why he hadn't been able to keep his eyes open long enough to kiss her again.

She couldn't stop herself from handing back a waspish reply. "I unzipped you so that you would be more comfortable. Satisfied? So now that we have that settled, if you think you can sit upright long enough to eat your food—without falling asleep and landing face first in it—I have bacon and eggs ready."

With that, she plunked his plate onto the small dinette table, unwound the dishtowel from around her neck and dropped it onto the countertop beside her. She then stalked off to get her own shower. And to set her muddled brain back on the right track before the long day ahead of her...and to hopefully keep it off the most perfect piece of male anatomy she'd ever seen.

Round and round and round she goes, where she stops nobody knows.

Lucas felt like he'd been pedaling the ergometer for hours, his hands moving in slow painful circles, his shoulder catching at a certain spot with every turn of the wheel. Where the hell was that physical therapist anyway? He'd hoped to at least have a couple more days to rest before Sophia dragged him down to the rehab center to start on his recovery regimen. He had a feeling it was because she didn't want to leave him in Marcos's apartment by himself.

What exactly did she expect him to do? Pitch head first off the balcony and land on the sidewalk below?

She was taking the doctor's orders a little too seriously. Besides, she'd been tense and irritable all morning, and he had no idea why. He suspected it had something to do with what had happened between them last night, but when he'd tried to talk about it on the short drive over to the hospital, she'd shut him down before he'd got six words out.

Surely she didn't want to forget that kiss ever happened, because he sure didn't.

It had been hot and wet and erotic. And that had been before she'd even opened her mouth and let him in.

After that…

He'd been a goner, because between her lips lay the thing a man's dreams were made of. So slick and—

"Ai, Senhor Carvalho! Cuidado!"

The warning had come from in front of him, and he realized the whine of the machine had increased along with the speed of his strokes, and his shoulder was now a quivering mass of burning rubber.

He let go of the pedals, cradling his arm as he let the machine come to a halt on its own. "I wasn't…" He wasn't what? Able get his mind off what it would have been like to have Sophia straddle him in an entirely different way?

"This was supposed to be a warm-up, not the main event." The therapist tsked at him. "Do you wish to damage your shoulder before we even start?"

Start? As far as he was concerned, they were done here.

But Greta—from Sweden—had other ideas. She worked his butt—and every other part of him—until he swore his skin would peel back and expose the muscle fibers underneath.

When she was finally finished with him, Lucas slumped in a chair in the waiting area, wanting nothing more than to curl into a ball and block out the world.

Only he didn't want Sophia to find him like that and tell him to get with the program. Because he was more than willing to, *if* he knew what the program was.

Greta-the-Terrible must have called her, though, and let her know the session was over because Sophia came around the corner ten minutes later looking as fresh as a daisy, while his T-shirt was plastered to his skin and his hair was stiff from sweat. He was ready for his second shower of the day, although he doubted he could manage it at the moment. And somehow it galled him that Sophia was right there to see his every weakness.

Why couldn't their initial introductions have

been made at the medical conference, before the shooting…when he'd still at least had a few witticisms left in him? Right now he felt drained of everything, even words.

"Ready?" The question was light and brimming with cheer—nothing like her attitude from this morning. In fact, she flashed him a smile that seemed to come way too easily.

For some reason, it rubbed him the wrong way. "You stay and work. I'll take a taxi back to Marcos's place."

"No need. I've already found someone to fill in for me for the rest of the day."

Great. The last thing he needed right now was a babysitter, when all he wanted was to be left alone to lick his wounds. "Look. I know you told the doctor you'd stay at the apartment, but I'm sure he didn't mean for you to trail after me like a puppy every second of the day."

The words came from an ugly, hurting place inside him, and even as they spewed out he knew they were a mistake. Her face confirmed it, changing in the space of a few heartbeats, her smile freezing into an icy mask.

Her chin jerked up and she met his eyes without a flinch. "Have it your way, Dr. Carvalho.

This *puppy* knows when it's time to leave." She backed away.

"Wait, Sophia." He struggled to his feet. "I didn't mean it like that."

He succeeded in grabbing her wrist before she reached the door, his shoulder blaring out a warning. To his left he saw Greta throw him a frown and take a step in their direction. He let go, holding his hands away from his sides, palms facing out. "Don't leave. It's just hard for me to… I'm not used to relying on anyone."

And that was the truth.

The few childhood memories that had stuck with him had been of Marcos—a mini-warrior— who had always had to do everything just right, taking care of everyone around him. He'd been a tyrant, even kicking off his flip-flops and ordering Lucas to put them on because he'd been worried about him cutting his bare feet. What about Marcos's feet? Who'd worried about those?

Lucas had chafed under his watchful eye, had fought back every time his brother had sacrificed something on his behalf.

He hadn't needed it. Hadn't wanted it. He could take care of himself.

That battle cry had become ingrained. Once

he'd gone to live with his adoptive parents, the trend had continued. They'd tried to do things for him, had made sacrifices for him—perhaps trying to make up for the poverty of his childhood—and he'd fought against them, the need to be fiercely independent hardening into a cement-like substance that was almost impossible to break through.

It infuriated him that he couldn't get up and stroll out of the hospital—or get into a vehicle and haul his ass back to the apartment by himself. But that didn't mean he had to take his frustrations out on Sophia. Or anyone else.

He glanced back to make sure Greta wasn't going to come over and clobber him then moved forward another step. "I'm sore and tired, and I'm being extremely ungrateful. I'm sorry."

Her expression held steady for another moment before thawing around the edges. She released a small sigh, shoulders relaxing. "I'm sorry, too. I overreacted. Do you want me to drive you home?"

Home.

Lucas couldn't remember the last time he'd thought of anything by that term. He'd always been a drifter, too streetwise to put down roots, fearful they might be ripped up at any moment.

He had no home. No country—his trip to Brazil just seemed to re-emphasize that point.

He didn't know what he'd expected to find during this trip, but there'd been no burning sense of belonging. No flash of patriotic pride. No real sense of recognition, even when he'd seen Marcos for the first time in thirty years.

Maybe he was incapable of those kinds of feelings. Maybe that's why he traveled from city to city during his vacations under the guise of helping others.

No. That wasn't right, either. He got an immense amount of satisfaction from helping children who had little more than the barest of necessities. Kids who might not get a chance for a normal life without surgery.

Kids like Sophia had once been. She was the perfect example of what cosmetic surgery could do to improve someone's quality of life.

He glanced at the woman who was waiting patiently for his answer. "Yes, I think I'm more than ready to go."

Sophia had no idea what had caused his sudden shift in attitude, but her heart felt like it had cracked in half as he'd stood there and asked her not to go.

He may not have heard the note of pleading in his voice, but she had. And it brought back memories of when he'd been taken from the home. The way he'd pleaded for the young couple to let Marcos and Sophia come too. Of course he wouldn't remember any of that. And he hadn't been there to witness his brother's raw grief afterwards.

But it had cut her to the quick back then, just as his words had done a few seconds ago.

Once back at the apartment, Lucas dropped onto the leather ottoman and tried to lean over to undo his tennis shoes, only to sit up again, pain and exhaustion etched on his face. Sophia knelt in front of him and reached for the first shoe, ignoring his attempts to brush her hands away as she untied the laces and pulled it and his sock off. She repeated the act with the other foot. When she reached for the bottom of his T-shirt the muscles in his jaw went dangerously tight, but he let her tug it over his head without a word.

Deus. She tried not to stare, but her eyes skipped quickly over his torso, absorbing the smooth skin, the olive coloring showing off his Brazilian heritage to perfection.

The men she'd dated in the past had had this same olive skin, but the resemblance went no deeper than that. Neither of her other two lovers had carried the dangerous undertones that this man did. They'd been gentle and kind—and had avoided her lip like the plague. There was no pretense with Lucas. She had a feeling he took exactly what he wanted—said exactly what he pleased.

And if he wanted her?

She shook off the thought, realizing he was still sitting there without a shirt. Time to finish what she'd started.

She reached toward his belt, only to have him stagger to his feet. "I can manage the rest of it myself." As if realizing his words had come out with a hard edge, he added, "Thanks. I'm just going to shower and lie down for a while."

"Do you want some pain medicine?"

"Don't need it." As he walked away, Sophia frowned after him. He'd refused to take anything the last time she asked either, even though she'd known he'd been hurting like crazy. She'd heard of doctors who wouldn't go near any type of narcotics, but his words about not relying on anyone came back to her.

Maybe it wasn't just people he wasn't used to needing, but everything. Including pain pills.

While he slept, she took the opportunity to catch up on some emails and do some dusting and light housework. She had no idea if Marcos planned on bringing Maggie back with him or what was going on with their relationship, but she had a feeling wedding bells might be ringing before very long.

Marcos had never been one to dilly-dally. When he wanted something, he went after it. And he'd wanted Maggie. As much as Maggie had wanted him.

As happy as she was for her childhood friend, she couldn't wait for him to come back to São Paulo. It would be a relief not to be alone with Lucas day after day. Once home, Marcos could take over helping his brother, and she could quietly slip out of the picture, unnoticed and unmissed.

Her chest tightened at the thought.

No more kisses. No more anything.

She glanced at the hall, tempted to tiptoe back to the bedroom to make sure he was all right while she still could—to make sure he'd managed the shower on his own. From her perch on the sofa she saw the bedroom door was open, but it felt too peeping-Tom-ish to move closer. Besides, after the scene in the kitchen this morning, she was going to let him take care of his own sleeping arrangements from now on—she wouldn't be the one to cover him up or slide a pillow under his head.

Neither would she be unzipping his pants any time in the foreseeable future.

Yeah, well, even in the *un*foreseeable future, that wasn't going to happen. If that little metal tab had proved dangerous when the man was asleep, just imagine what would happen if she touched it while he was awake.

Deus.

That thought was best left behind if she hoped to make it through the next week or so unscathed—a prospect that seemed less and less likely. Because right now her emotions were showing some definite signs of wear and tear. One wrong move and they could rip apart at the seams. If that happened, even a plastic surgeon as talented as Lucas might not be able to stitch her back together.

CHAPTER EIGHT

Sophia pulled the curtain around Sílvio Airton's bed and prepared to check his vitals.

"How are you feeling today?"

Sílvio, a sweet elderly gentleman who'd joked with the staff for the last couple of days, had been battling renal failure for months. He'd been hospitalized several times in recent weeks with infections that came and went and had had a bout of pneumonia last January.

His relatives knew one of these visits would be Sílvio's last but everyone—Sophia included—hoped he would rally once again, like he'd done on previous occasions.

"I'm getting pretty tired of being poked and prodded." The words were delivered with a smile, despite the fact that dialysis wasn't a pleasant event. But without it Sílvio wouldn't have a chance.

And with a new grandbaby due in less than

a week, he wasn't quite ready to throw in the towel yet.

She patted his shoulder. "I know. Just hang in there, okay?" Pushing up the sleeve on his hospital gown and wrapping the rubber tourniquet around his upper arm, she got ready to do a blood draw. "So, is Jesse having a girl or a boy?"

By now, Sophia was on a first-name basis with most of Sílvio's relatives.

"They want it to be a surprise."

His veins were fragile, and Sophia took special care to try to get the needle in on the first attempt.

There. Blood flowed into the vial, and as soon as the tube was full she popped it off and attached a second one. "Surprises can be fun."

Well, some of them anyway. She'd thrown herself into her job over the last couple of days due to just such a surprise. She hadn't quite decided if that kiss fell into the good category or the bad. What she did know was there was an awful ache of need that was steadily growing inside her.

The result of seeing Lucas all too often, because she was still spending each night at the apartment—rearranging her schedule to drive him back and forth to his therapy sessions.

In fact, untying his tennis shoes and helping

him out of his shirt afterwards had become almost sacred rituals. Watching him rise from that ottoman like a god—lithe and strong—muscles pumped full of blood from his workout, made her feel weak in the knees. She tried to make sure she'd scrambled to her feet before he got up, because having that pesky zipper at eye level made her want to extend her ministrations to other areas.

Well, she wouldn't be taking off his shoes—or anything else—for much longer. As soon as he got the all-clear from his doctor, she was out of the apartment and out of his life. Why? Because it was getting harder and harder to keep her mind—and hands—off Marcos's brother.

Make that impossible. And she had no idea why.

For his part, Lucas seemed oblivious to her inner turmoil. For that she was thankful. He hadn't tried to kiss her again or given any indication that he even wanted to if the opportunity were to arise.

And it had.

Almost every time she hauled his shirt over his head, he could have reached out and had her writhing beneath him in a matter of minutes. He'd never made a move.

Yep. Very grateful.

Mixed in with that relief, however, was a strange sense of disappointment. She felt flat. Out of sorts.

Sonia, one of Sílvio's adult children, peered around the curtain just as she was affixing labels on the sides of the blood samples. "How's he doing?"

Sophia smiled and waved the woman in. She went straight to the bed and kissed her dad on the cheek. A lump gathered in her throat at the obvious affection between the two. This was what parent-child relationships were supposed to be like.

"He's just getting ready to head to dialysis." Sticking the vials of blood in the holder, she peeled off her gloves. "I hear Jesse is getting close to term."

The woman grinned. "Yes, we keep hoping she'll deliver just a little early." She glanced at her dad, and there was a wealth of meaning in her look. She hoped her father would live to see the birth of his grandchild.

The lump in her throat grew. "Well, you'll have to keep me posted."

An orderly appeared around the corner with a wheelchair. "You have a patient for me?"

When he saw who it was, the man grinned. "Ah, Senhor Airton. You're just the man I was hoping to see today. So, what's the newest piece of government gossip?"

Sílvio had been a politician in his younger days and had his own set of opinions on just about every subject, but he delivered them with a wit and humor that disarmed even those who weren't of the same political bent.

As usual, the two got into a good-natured discussion as the orderly helped Sílvio into the chair and took off down the hall. Sonia gave a quick roll of her eyes, before waving and hurrying after them.

As Sophia headed back to her desk, she wondered if the woman knew just how lucky she was to have a large and loving family. Or Lucas, for that matter, who'd had people who'd loved him enough to take him in and give him a home.

As if he knew she'd been thinking about him, he came strolling down the hallway much earlier than he should have and crooked a finger at her. She frowned. He didn't look tired. Or sweaty. Could he have showered before he'd left the therapy area?

Faint disappointment slashed through her, making her wince. Great. All those thoughts about being glad when this was over? Lies. She *wasn't* glad. She wanted to rip that shirt off his body just to prove her point.

She curled her fingers into her palms to stop them from getting any bright ideas then forced herself to move towards him, her shoes making almost no sound on the polished floor. "Are you done already?"

"GTT is sick today, so I'm off the hook."

Her brows went up. "GTT?"

"Greta-the-Terrible."

She laughed. "Very mature, Dr. Carvalho. I suppose you have a witty moniker for everyone."

"Of course." He leaned closer with a conspiratorial whisper. "Want to know what yours is?"

"I don't think so." Another lie. But Lucas didn't have to know that.

"It fits you to a T."

She gave a mock sigh, his woodsy masculine scent doing a number on her insides. "Oh, okay. What is it?"

"Sophia-the-Sweet."

Sarcasm. Just what she needed today. "I thought it might be Sophia-the-Slave-Driver."

"Slave-driver. Mmm. I kind of like the sound of that."

Deus! All kinds of images popped into her

head. Bad images. "So you're not having therapy at all today?"

"I'm supposed to work on it at home." He propped a shoulder against the wall. "So I came down to ask a favor."

"You need me to drive you to the apartment? It's a little early, but I'll see if I can find—"

"No, no. I don't need you to take me home. I need you to remove my stitches."

She blinked. "What?"

"I was supposed to have them out the other day after therapy, but I had that meltdown, and then didn't want to ask you to drive me back to the hospital."

Sophia counted through the days that had passed since his surgery. How had she lost track of time? "That therapy session was three days ago."

He gave a quick shrug that said it was no big deal. "I could do the ones on my abdomen myself, but I can't get to the ones on my shoulder or snip them one-handed."

Her mouth popped open. "You are *not* going to take out your own stitches."

"Well, it's either that or…ask you to do it." He gave her a slow smile. "If Sophia-the-Sweet can come out to play, that is."

Ah, so that's where the name had come from. He was buttering her up.

Great. The last thing she wanted to do was "come out to play"—or lay her hands on his bare abdomen, for that matter. "We could call the doctor and set up another appointment. I'm sure he's going to want to have a look at it anyway."

"Come on, Sophia. It'll take maybe ten minutes at the most. If it looks like there's a problem, we'll call the doctor and have him check it. As it is, the edges of the incisions look sealed, and I'm doing my therapy without any problems."

"I'm still having to help you get undressed afterwards."

"Yes. You are. Which is why this should be no big deal. What do you say?"

She swallowed. This man was turning out to be a whole lot more work than she'd bargained for. And it had nothing to do with physical work— it was her emotions that were feeling the strain. "Fine. Let me tell someone where I'll be."

A few minutes later they were in one of the exam rooms and she had his chart out. Against his wishes, she'd made a quick phone call to his doctor to make sure it was okay for her to remove the sutures. Once she'd got the go-ahead she laid out all the items she'd need and motioned for him to take off his shirt.

Instead, he held his arms up.

Oh, Lord. That's right. He couldn't do it on his own. She glanced at the closed door.

What have you let yourself get talked into, Sophia?

She gingerly grabbed hold of the bottom of his shirt and pushed it up his torso. There was a quick wince as he lowered his injured arm, rotated his shoulder.

She gave her own little wince as the familiar smooth tissue and subtly defined muscle groups came into view. He didn't have the overly developed body of someone who worked out all the time, but he was firm in all the right places, his biceps curved and strong, his stomach taut and flat. The light dusting of hair narrowed once it left his chest, running down in a straight line and disappearing into his pants. But she knew first hand his zipper followed that narrow trail as well.

And that was her cue to cut her glance back to his face and get on with her job. When she did so, however, there was a glimmer of amusement in his eyes. "I thought only men had that problem."

"What problem is that?"

"Not quite knowing where to look."

Her face heated, but she somehow found a quip to match his. "Funny, because I thought I was examining your stitches."

Ha! Since her glance had skipped right over the pucker of flesh partially visible above his waistband, that was about as close to a fib as she could get.

"Of course you were."

He knew. The man knew she'd been enjoying the view!

She plunked a metal tray beside him, instruments rattling in protest. "Do you want those stitches out, or should I call the doctor?"

He reached for her wrist and tugged her forward. "I'd much prefer you do it."

Why now? Why was he flirting—and, yes, he was definitely flirting—with her in a public place, when he'd totally ignored her back at the apartment? She couldn't figure him out.

"Then let me get started." She was not up to playing word games with this man—now or ever. Not when his skills in that department far outranked hers, which were pretty much non-existent.

He let go of her, a slight frown marring his brow

as he reached up to tuck back a lock of hair that had fallen over her cheek. "I'm sorry, Sophia. I keep forgetting you're from a different world."

A different world. As in the poor little orphan girl no one had wanted? Not even him?

There were times he seemed to be attracted to her. But it was probably just because there was no one else. He was stuck here in Brazil for a couple more weeks, and she was available—you couldn't get much more available than sharing an apartment. Except he hadn't been interested enough to actually go further than a kiss. Not without falling asleep.

Why that had bothered her so much, she wasn't sure.

"You're right," she said. "We are from different worlds. Better for us both to remember that."

He leaned back and studied her face, his own features shifting from lazy amusement to closed and shuttered in a few brief seconds. He nodded. "Point taken. Okay, let's get this over with."

Her heart in her stomach, she sluiced alcohol onto a piece of gauze and carefully wiped down his shoulder, deciding to go from easy to hard. Sliding her fingers across his abdomen was definitely going to be the more difficult of the two areas. She took the tweezers and carefully gripped the first knotted suture and pulled it taut, snipping it close to the incision line and sliding it free of his skin. Doing the same for the next five stitches, she kept her attention focused on the task at hand, snipping and dropping each section of suture material into the basin. When all the stitches were out, she examined the site, then wiped it down one more time with a fresh piece of gauze.

"I want to put a couple pieces of tape across it to make sure your movements don't pull anything open."

"It should be closed by now."

"Humor me." She gave him a smile, although it was a little shakier than she liked. Cutting two pieces of surgical tape, she laid them perpendicular to the direction of his incision, pulling them snug to absorb some of the stress that came with moving his arm.

"You know that'll come off the first time it gets wet, don't you?"

She ignored him and took a deep breath before facing the stitches on his abdomen. Damn. She so didn't want to undo his pants, but with part of the sutures hidden beneath his waistband there wasn't a choice.

"I need you to—"

"Got it." He undid the button and edged the zipper down an inch or two. He peeled one side away until the rest of the incision came into view. "Will that do?"

"Perfect." Also perfect was the fact that he had on a pair of black briefs.

When her gloved hand lightly touched him, his abdominal muscles contracted, and he drew in a hissed breath. But when she looked up, he gave her a tight smile. "Tickles."

If only that was all she felt when she touched him. But, no, it was a whole lot more complicated than that, and she wasn't quite sure how to deal with it other than to just hurry and finish what she was doing. Following the same sequence, she sanitized the area and reached for the tweezers again, noting the muscles were still rigid against her fingers. Still tickling? Was he afraid she'd nick him with the scissors? She wasn't about to ask so she went to work, snipping the stitches one by one from the surgical site.

"Are you hanging in there?"

"Just finish up, will you?"

She glanced up to see his jaw was as stiff as his abs, the skin pulled tight over his cheekbones. Was she hurting him?

She was being as careful as possible. Still, she slowed her movements, just in case. "Only a few more to go."

He didn't answer, just waited until she tugged the last stitch free and dropped it into the basin. "There. All done."

His muscles went slack all at once, backbone curving as he leaned forward, forearms resting along his thighs. He drew a long shaky breath, then let it out with a muffled curse.

Something was wrong. He hadn't even given her a chance to pass over the site with more rubbing alcohol.

Alarmed, she touched his shoulder. "Lucas, are you okay?"

"Just give me a minute, will you?"

"Why? Are you in pain?" Maybe something was going on with the repair the surgeon had done on his liver. "Let me see—"

"Dammit, Sophia." He shook off her hand. "I'm trying to do the right thing here."

"I don't understand. Did I hurt you?"

"Yes, that's exactly it. It hurts. But not in the way you think." He finally looked up, and the heat blazing in his eyes made her breath catch in her throat. "And if you say one more word in the next thirty seconds I swear I'm going to lay you down on this exam table and show you exactly what I mean by that."

She couldn't keep her eyes from shooting down to a certain area of his anatomy to see if he was saying what she thought he was.

Oh! How had she missed *that*?

Despite his seated position, the seam of his slacks bulged in a way that could only mean one thing. Within seconds, a certain part of her had an equal and opposite reaction, going soft and liquid, preparing to receive whatever he had to give. And if that meant being sprawled beneath him on that table then so be it.

A shiver went over her, starting at her head and rippling all the way down to her toes.

She opened her mouth to speak, praying she made it before her thirty seconds were up.

The sound hadn't even exited her throat when the exam-room door swung wide and a male voice behind her said, "Dr. Carvalho, sorry to bother you. Someone said you were in here. I think we have something that might interest you." There was a second or two of silence that seemed to stretch to eternity. "Am I interrupting something?"

Sophia's mouth snapped shut like a clam that suddenly realized the world was a much more dangerous place than it expected.

Lucas never took his eyes off her. "Nurse Limeira was just taking out my stitches. I'll be right with you."

The second the door closed behind the departing doctor, Lucas slid off the table coming within inches of touching her. "Were you about to say something to me?"

She shook her head, allowing her silence to speak for her.

Cupping her cheek, his thumb whispered across her lower lip. It gave a fatal tremble that gave her away.

"I think you're lying. The question is whether it's for your benefit or for mine." He gave her a slow, devastating grin as he dropped his hand and took a step back. "You may think you dodged a bullet here, Sophia. But one day very soon either your luck is going to run out or my good intentions are going to fail me. When either of those things happen…honey, make no mistake. It won't be on a hard metal table or done in a rush. And most important of all, there'll be no interruptions."

CHAPTER NINE

Lucas tried to keep his mind on the procedure from his perch high above the operating room.

Dr. Guilherme Lima sat beside him in the observation area. "I figured you'd want to see the new technique in action." Young and fresh-faced, the other doctor glanced over at him. "Also, your brother called a few minutes ago and wanted me to check in on you. He'd tried to call Sophia, but couldn't get an answer."

He hadn't heard her cellphone ring. Then again, he didn't think she'd had her purse with her when she'd followed him into the exam room to remove his stitches. Ringtones hadn't exactly been at the forefront of his mind, however, because he could have sworn Sophia had been about to respond to the challenge he'd thrown down. If he were a betting man, he'd go all in that she had been going to call his bluff.

Only he hadn't been bluffing. He'd been so hard and ready in those endless moments as her hands had trailed over his body that he'd been prepared to grab her and do exactly what he'd threatened to do: lay her over that table and show her exactly what she did to him.

Had she been about to accept?

Just thinking about it made his flesh react all over again.

Get your mind back on the surgery, Carvalho or everyone in this hospital is going to know exactly where things stand between you and Sophia.

Hell, not even *he* knew where they stood. All he knew was that she was killing him. Just by looking at him.

And her touch...

Deadly. Just like a hemorrhagic fever that ripped through the body with little warning, taking no captives.

He was toast.

His mind wandered to her lips and the silky skin he'd stroked thirty minutes earlier.

He glanced at the doctor beside him. "If a child from one of the local orphanages came in with a cleft lip, who would do the repair? You?"

"An orphanage?" The man's brows went up. "That kind of thing is handled through one of the public hospitals in São Paulo. Why?"

"Just thinking." Aware the other man was now staring at him, he went on, "I do charity work from time to time."

Somehow he didn't feel as much of a sense of pride in saying those words as he might have at one time because now he had a living, breathing example of someone he might have worked on had she been born in Africa or Mexico.

The young surgeon turned to look at him. "I could put you in touch with someone, if you want to know how that kind of thing works here. I did an internship at the Hospital de Santa Maria a few years back."

A few years back. This kid didn't look like he was out of his twenties yet, much less had been practicing medicine for more than a year or two. Suddenly, at thirty-four, Lucas felt old and unsettled.

But he didn't want to be settled. That was the whole point of his travels. He never wanted to be tied down. Stuck in one spot.

Nope. That wasn't true. He was *afraid* to be tied down. There was a world of difference between those two concepts. Despite the stability his adoptive parents had provided, he'd never really felt a true sense of "place." He'd been ripped from the only home he'd ever known and placed in an orphanage. Then his new parents, even though they hadn't meant to, had taken the rest of his identity away from him, including his brother and his last name. Including Sophia, who he'd never gotten the chance to know. Not really.

Weirdly, he was jealous of his brother because he'd had what he himself hadn't.

That in itself made him feel like a jerk. He'd been given everything, and yet he was coveting the one thing his brother had that Lucas didn't: Sophia's affection.

Hell, he'd had the world handed to him on a silver platter, and he still wasn't satisfied.

What did that make him?

Greedy.

Was that what was behind the persistent salute one part of his body kept giving Sophia? Was he enough of an animal that he felt the need to "mark" her and claim her as his—just to show his brother that she would have chosen him over Marcos during their time at the orphanage?

If so, he didn't like that side of himself very much because it meant he wasn't really interested in Sophia as a person but in taking what his brother had.

He glanced over at the doctor whose attention was wholly on the breast reduction surgery being done in the room below. The surgeon was currently making impossibly tiny stitches along the bottom curve of the woman's breast. Lucas couldn't help but admire the skill it took to keep that up for hours on end. No quick stapling of skin here, the other doctor had told him. Plastic surgeons in Brazil felt there was a fine art to making small precise stitches that left a minimal scar.

That was one thing they could agree on. Lucas tended to dislike staples as well. But he'd told Sophia the truth when he'd said he wasn't interested in this side of plastic surgery.

"I think I would like the name of your contact at the public hospital, if the offer's still open."

"Of course." The other doctor pulled his smartphone from his pocket and scrolled through the screens. "What's your email, and I'll send it to you? Speaking of charity work, you know that Marcos opened a free clinic in one of the *favelas*, right?"

"No, I didn't. Which *favela*?"

"The one right down the hill."

The place he'd been born. And the place he'd been shot. Had Marcos been there that day? He'd never mentioned anything about a clinic or working down there. Not that there'd been much time to discuss anything before he'd headed for the States.

Lucas recited his email address, his eyes still on the meticulous procedure going on below them.

His memories of the shooting were coming back in drips and drabs—standing on a hill overlooking the *favela*, the dilapidated shacks that seemed to stretch endlessly into the distance. The sounds of shouting, the police running up the hill after a group of men. The shots. Falling to the ground.

Sophia's sweet smile as he'd recovered from his surgery.

His memories weren't the only improvements he saw. His muscles were responding to therapy as well, growing stronger over the last week. Soon he'd be able to drive again. Fly home. The police would be able to handle the investigation without any help from him, leaving him free to take up life where he'd left off.

He frowned. Why did that thought suddenly fill him with anything but relief? He should be glad to get out of this place. To get back to the States.

Sophia's face swam in his head, her features murky and indistinct as they wavered in and out of focus. For just a second he thought he saw the image of a little girl with dark, short-cropped hair and huge eyes superimposed over that picture. As soon as he blinked, however, it was gone. And no matter how hard he concentrated or tried to bring it back into view, just like his childhood with his father and brother, it was lost to him for ever.

"Why are we here?" Sophia had to raise her voice as she glanced around the doctor's waiting room, which was housed inside one of the largest public hospitals in Brazil. Half-broken toys were shoved in a corner, while every chair in the place was occupied by an adult with a child.

A shiver went over her. How different would her life have been had her parents been able to bring her to a place like this? Instead, they'd left her at the orphanage and let someone else deal with her disfigurement.

She scrubbed the thought away, leaning against a nearby wall and trying not to face the reality before her. The one time she'd glanced around the room she'd been struck by the chaotic activity, but even louder than the noise was the hope and fear etched on each adult's face, while the children did what kids did best. Laughed, cried, threw temper tantrums, totally unaware that there was something wrong with them. At least in the eyes of the world.

"This is what I do when I'm not at my hospital, working." Lucas leaned closer in order to be heard.

She gave him an incredulous look. "So, when you're not working, you're…working."

He shrugged. "I don't have anyone or anything tying me down. I figure it's one way to pass the time."

Nice to know that's how he felt about people like her. She'd merely been a way to pass someone's time.

A brush of fingers touched her wrist. "That's not true," he said, lowering his voice. "This is something I've always felt the need to do." Then his hand reached up and scrubbed at his arm. The spot where she knew the tattoo of his father was inked. "For him. For people like him who have no one to turn to."

She nodded. That she could understand.

Just as she started to say something else, a tiny girl crawled towards them, head down as she powered her way across the room. Around eight months old and clad only in a diaper, she was followed closely by a woman who had to be her mother. When the child lifted her head, Sophia saw that she had a bilateral cleft, a line running from each nostril down to her upper lip. Her mom murmured an apology and scooped the child up. When she started to move away, Sophia stopped her, leaning over to smile at the child, who immediately responded with a wide smile, the problem with her mouth doing nothing to dim the happiness in her eyes.

"She's beautiful. Is she yours?" She didn't know why she asked the question, maybe because her own folks hadn't been around to see her through surgery.

"Thank you. And, yes, she is." The woman spoke Portuguese, but her accent was different. Angolan, maybe? That might explain why the baby was a little older than most infants who had this type of surgery—although if her palate was cleft as well, that could be the reason, as those repairs were sometimes done later to give the bony plates time to grow.

Lucas brushed the backs of his knuckles over the baby's cheek, giving her a smile as well, although his eyes were sharp as he studied her. Seeing how he would approach the surgery maybe?

Just then the door to the back opened and a nurse appeared, clipboard in hand, and called a name. The woman in front of them smiled. "Well, that's for us. Wish us luck."

"Of course," Sophia murmured, not sure what else to say. But when the woman turned to leave, Sophia again reached out to stop her. The young mother turned back, and Sophia touched her own lip. "You're going to be so happy you had this done."

The woman's eyes widened. "You? You've had…"

"Yes. Many years ago." She hesitated then quickly dug into her purse for a card. "If you need anyone to talk to, please call me."

The woman accepted the slip of paper then reached down and clasped Sophia's hand, giving it a squeeze. "Thank you so much."

With that, she turned and went to the door where the nurse stood, and the trio disappeared. Soon the woman's baby would have a whole new look, but more than that, her future would be much brighter than it would have been had she not had surgery.

Fingers threaded through hers, and she looked up in surprise as Lucas pressed their joined hands against the warmth of his leg. "That was nice of you."

"I always wonder if my parents would have made a different decision had they had the money or a good support system in place."

He frowned. "What do you mean, a different decision? I thought they passed away."

"No. Why would you think that?"

His hand tightened around hers. "I just assumed…"

Oh. She got it. She'd been raised in an orphanage, so therefore her parents must have been tragically killed in a car accident. Or died by some other means. Like his and Marcos's parents had.

She shook her head. "Not all children in orphanages are actually orphans. My parents are still very much alive." She shrugged. "It's no big deal. Some people just can't afford to raise a child—especially one with medical issues. So…they send them away instead."

CHAPTER TEN

NO BIG DEAL.

Lucas couldn't believe she'd actually used those words. Being abandoned by parents who were supposed to love you was a huge deal. His dad had been as poor as dirt and yet he'd done the best he could…had kept his boys by his side until the day he'd died.

He had a feeling that if she'd been talking about any other child she'd have been furious. Just like he was now. As he sat in the doctor's office, listening while the pediatric surgeon talked about the various patients he saw, his gut did a slow, angry burn.

He'd had an hour to digest the fact that Sophia wasn't an actual orphan before they'd been called back to the doctor's office.

No. She *was* an orphan. Just because her biological father and mother were still on this planet, it didn't make them parents. In any way, shape or form.

Did she still have contact with them? Were they lost to her the way Marcos had been to him for many of his formative years?

He hoped Sophia had washed her hands of them, hoped they never got to share a single one of her special milestones. They didn't deserve it.

She half turned towards him then touched his knee. It was then he realized the doctor had asked him a question.

"I'm sorry. I missed that."

"I asked where you practice." Older, with a slightly stooped posture, Dr. Figuereiro's eyes glimmered with a trace of humor and sharp intelligence.

Lucas forced himself to tune back into the conversation. The plastic surgeon had given up valuable time to speak with them. He didn't deserve to sit there while *his* damn mind wandered all over the place. "My actual medical practice is in California, but I travel to Africa and Mexico whenever possible."

"That must be very rewarding work."

It was, but Dr. Figuereiro's work must be rewarding as well. He nodded at the wall where photo after photo was tacked to a giant corkboard.

There were so many images that they overlapped. "Are these all your patients?"

"Yes." He smiled as he swiveled his chair to glance at the wall. "These are my kids. It never fails to bring a lump to my throat whenever a parent sends me updates."

Sophia shifted next to him, and his heart cramped in his chest.

Some parents sent nothing at all. As soon as they left the office, he was going to ask her what happened. Had her parents abandoned her before or after the surgery?

Before. He would almost bet on it.

As casually as possible, he laid his hand on the back of her chair, needing to touch her but not willing to make it as obvious as holding her hand. Instead, he slid his fingers beneath her curtain of hair, where the doctor couldn't see, and used his thumb to stroke across the back of her neck. She sat up a bit straighter but didn't try to shift or pull away.

"We saw an older baby out in the waiting room," he said. "Do you often get them so late?"

The man pursed his lips. "When they can't get what they need in their own countries, they're forced to go elsewhere. We're only one of several places that accept cases like hers."

Sophia cleared her throat. "Your waiting room was packed earlier."

"It's like that every day. We deal with all kinds of craniofacial problems, not just cleft lips and palates."

His focus shifted to Sophia. "Your repair is excellent, by the way. How long ago was it done?"

Sophia shrugged. "I was a little older as well, about a year old. So thirty-three years or so ago."

"You had it done here in São Paulo?"

"Yes. I grew up at Saint Mary's over in the *Dutra* area."

"I've worked on kids from that home for many years." Dr. Figuereiro pulled his glasses down from the top of his head and perched them on his nose. He glanced at her over the top of them. "Would you be offended if I took a look?"

"No, of course not."

Standing and coming around to their side of the desk, he took hold of Sophia's hand, signaling her to get up and forcing Lucas to drop his arm from around her shoulders.

Once she was on her feet, the doctor peered closely at her lip, tucking his hand beneath her chin and turning her face to different angles. Lucas was fine until the man touched the scar itself then his gut tightened, a ball of some strange emotion turning round and round until everything inside him was all jumbled up. Sophia, on the other hand, seemed unfazed by the intimate touch.

Yet when *he'd* touched it, she'd tensed immediately, claiming he made her feel self-conscious about it. But why? He did the exact same type of surgery all the time, so why was she so nonchalant about someone else touching her?

"Thirty-three years… I think I may have done this repair." He let go of her and gazed up at the ceiling, as if doing some quick calculations in his head. He glanced at Lucas. "Which technique do you use when dealing with unilateral clefts?"

"A variation of Millard's rotation."

"Yes, I was beginning to use Millard's right about the time your young lady was having her surgery done. She had a good outcome. I'm glad."

Lucas's brain ceased to function after the "your young lady" comment.

Sophia quickly shook her head. "Oh, we're not together. I'm helping Dr. Carvalho recover from surgery." She added, "In a professional capacity only."

The surgeon glanced from one to the other with a quirk of his brow. "Interesting." He patted her on the shoulder. "Well, thank you for letting me look."

Sophia retook her seat. "If you did the surgery on me, I'm forever grateful. Most people don't even notice my scar."

Was it his imagination or had her emphasis on the word "most" carried a slightly caustic inflection?

Dr. Figuereiro waved off her thanks. "It's what I'm here for. Although I don't think I have many more years of surgery left in me. I'm about at the age where it's time to pass the baton on to the next man in line."

"What'll happen to your patients?" Lucas asked. "Are there other doctors willing to take on those from lower socioeconomic levels?"

If his father had found a doctor as caring as this one, he might still be alive. It made Lucas all the more aware of how different Sophia's life could have been had she not gotten a top-notch surgeon like Dr. Figuereiro.

"Are there others who are willing? I hope so. It

takes someone who's in it for the right reasons." He smiled. "Interested in the job?"

Something in his chest leaped at the thought before he forced the emotion back. He laughed instead, pretending he didn't know if the doctor was serious or not. "I bet you don't get many surgeons from other countries."

"To practice medicine, you mean?" He shook his head. "Not many. Most doctors working with NGOs head straight for the Amazon. Or Africa. With all the hospitals around here, São Paulo isn't exactly an exotic destination for medical teams. Why?"

"Just curious." He noted that Sophia avoided his glance and he didn't bother sliding his hand onto the back of her chair again. He certainly didn't want the good doctor to think there was anything going on between them, especially as he had no idea if Dr. Figuereiro and Marcos knew each other. The last thing he needed was for something to get back to his brother and set off a chain reaction that would be difficult to explain away.

Although Lucas certainly hadn't been worried about Marcos's reaction when he'd threatened to lay Sophia on the exam table and do her right there in the hospital. Of all the moronic things to have done, that was pretty much at the top of the list.

But he was thinking rationally now.

And he was going to do everything in his power to make sure he *kept* thinking with a clear head, no matter what crazy impulses his nervous system might send out. Like sticking around for a while? Definitely not a workable plan.

He stood, making sure to take it slow and easy as he reached across the desk to shake the good doc's hand. "Well, thank you for your time. You still have some folks waiting out there."

"My pleasure." The other doctor clasped his hand in a firm, unwavering grip, then stood as well. "Come back some time when we have time to exchange ideas on technique. Or if you get the urge to extend your visit indefinitely."

Indefinitely.

No. That wasn't happening. He couldn't see himself doing what Dr. Figuereiro did: work on someone like Sophia and then thirty years later still be in the same location. Even in the States he'd already practiced in two different cities and had volunteered in more than six countries. And even now something inside him was itching to move on to something new.

You wouldn't want those roots to suddenly start growing, right?

He decided to go with a noncommittal reply. "If I decide to, you'll be the first to know. How's that?"

"I won't hold my breath. How's that?" Another smile accompanied the words, and the doctor came around the desk as Sophia also got to her feet. He took hold of her shoulders then kissed her on the cheek in standard São Paulo fashion. "And you don't be a stranger either, young lady. I still have room on my cork board for another picture or two if you'd care to send one in."

She smiled. "I just might do that. Thank you again for having us." She paused. "Do you have a card? I'd like to give you a call some time."

To talk about her surgery?

Dr. Figeureiro went back around his desk and pulled open one of the battered side drawers. "If you ever want to come down the hill from that fancy hospital, I might be able to use another nurse. Or whoever takes over the practice might need one." He cast another sly glance in Lucas's direction.

Color seeped into Sophia's face right on cue as the doctor passed a card across the space. She accepted it, hurriedly stuffing it into her handbag.

Lucas was sure that was the last thing Sophia wanted, to work with someone who'd kissed her and then fallen asleep, someone who'd threatened to seduce her in a hospital room. Yeah. No wonder she'd turned red.

Once outside the office, they headed to her car. As they got in, Lucas pulled the seat belt across his shoulder, very thankful it wasn't his injured one. The lower part of the mechanism, however, was a different story. It crossed directly over where his stitches had been, and although the skin might have healed, it was still pretty sore. He glanced sideways to where she was twisting the key in the ignition. "Sorry about that, Sophia. I don't know why he thought there was something going on."

She didn't even look his way. "I can't imagine."

"Is something wrong?" She'd barely said two words the whole visit, other than asking for the doctor's card.

"Nope." She sat there for a moment, her fingers wrapped around the steering wheel. "I'm thinking about going home tomorrow, if you think you can handle things from here. I'll still come by and pick you up for your physical therapy appointments, and I can bring meals by if you need me to. But you seem to be pretty self-sufficient at this point."

All he heard was that she was going home.

Leaving.

His throat squeezed shut for several seconds before he forced it to relax so he could breathe normally.

What the hell was with that? Why did he care if she stayed or if she left? After all, he'd been "leaving" one place or another his entire life.

So why was hearing it from Sophia—who was not a permanent fixture in his life in any sense of the word—making him want to pretend to be a whole lot sicker than he was?

He had no idea. Maybe it was the crazy thought Dr. Figueriro had planted in his mind. His wandering heart was starting to kick into gear again with a new and exciting opportunity. But coming here to do anything would be a big mistake. That doctor's patients didn't need a temporary fixture. They needed someone they could count on to be there to see them through the hard times—tragic times. And to show those kids that someone really did care.

He didn't do that on his volunteer trips, and had never felt bad about it. But this was different. This was a community that saw too little stability—he, more than anyone, should understand that.

He forced his mind back to Sophia and her comment about leaving, noticing she hadn't made any move to pull out of the parking space and into traffic. Drawing a deep breath, he managed to say, "If that's what you think is best, that's what you should do."

"You'll be okay?"

"Absolutely." He kept his voice light, forcing into it a lazy amusement that he didn't feel at all.

"I'll leave you my cellphone number." She finally looked at him. "You can call me if you want or need anything."

Call her. If he wanted anything. Needed anything.

No way. No how.

He was not even going to think about the ramifications of that statement. He wouldn't call her, because if he did, it would be for one thing. To take her in his arms and drag her down the hallway of his brother's apartment until they were both sprawled across that huge king-sized bed of his.

What Lucas wanted and what he should have were two entirely different things, however. Maybe Sophia had finally wised up and realized the last place she should be was in the same house as him. Especially after what he'd nearly done in that hospital room. He couldn't promise her it wouldn't happen again. Because it would. Maybe not today, maybe not tomorrow. But soon.

That thought should shock him back to reality, but it didn't. It made the anticipation of kissing her—touching her—that much sharper.

Only one thing was stopping him from doing all the things he'd dreamed of doing to her, and that was Sophia herself. He didn't want to hurt her, but he knew if he slept with her there was a very real chance that he could. That he *would*. If that happened, Marcos would pummel him into the ground, and Lucas would stand there and let him do his worst—because he wouldn't be doing anything that Lucas wouldn't be doing to himself.

Sophia was sweet. Innocent. She didn't deserve to have someone screw around with her affections. Someone who had no intention of sticking around and making things permanent.

So he wouldn't call her. She was doing absolutely the right thing in running as far away from him as she could get.

But as much as he might believe that in his heart of hearts, at this moment it was the last thing Lucas wanted her to do.

CHAPTER ELEVEN

SHE DIDN'T WANT to go home today.

But asking Lucas to eat lunch at one of the city's famed *rodízios* was pretty pitiful as far as delaying tactics went. Maybe she hadn't expected him to capitulate to the idea of her leaving quite so easily. He had. Hadn't even blinked when she'd suggested moving out.

Sitting across from her in the steakhouse's dimly lit interior, her dining companion glanced around the place.

Dark wooden tables contrasted with the many white-suited servers, who traveled from table to table, each man laden with a different cut of meat, some on wheeling carts, other types carried on wide sword-like skewers.

"So how does this work exactly?" Lucas asked.

"How is it that you've never been to a *rodízio*? Your parents never took you to one? Not once?"

"We lived in the States for most of my life."

He shrugged. "Maybe they just never had the opportunity."

Sophia had thought him one of the lucky ones to have been adopted. But maybe she'd been wrong. His adoptive father was Brazilian, so it was hard to understand how he could speak Portuguese but not know how to order meat.

She tapped a wooden placard that sat in the middle of the table and showed him how to turn the knob that flipped a tab from red to green. "Green means you want them to bring meat to your table. Red means to stop. The word *rodízio* basically means 'making the rounds,' which is what the servers are doing. We normally try to have several different cuts on our plates before switching the sign to red. Then once you're ready to start again, you turn it back to green."

"No side dishes?"

She nodded towards the middle of the room where there was a long buffet table. "There's salad and vegetables over there, but most people come here for the meat."

"And how do you know which cut is which?"

She laughed. "Well, I can't help you with that, because I don't know the names in English. I can tell you what I like, and you can taste it and see if it appeals to you."

His fingers tightened on the knob for several seconds, eyes narrowing as he studied her face. "Oh, I'm pretty sure it would."

"You never know. Everyone has different tastes."

He leaned forward, his gaze unwavering. "I'm sure your taste would suit me just fine."

She sucked down a quick breath, suddenly aware that he'd taken her words the wrong way. She hadn't meant them to be risqué. But if he offered to taste her, she was going to be in big trouble, because she wasn't sure she'd be able to resist him.

Now, more than ever, she needed to keep her wits about her. "Um, let's turn it to green, shall we?"

"Let's." He flipped the lever and gave her a slow wicked smile. "Green for go."

Thankfully this place was efficient, so almost as soon as the card had been changed, a waiter came over with one of the shiny rotisserie skewers. "Filet mignon, *senhor*?"

Lucas nodded. "Now, *that* cut I understand, it's the same in both languages."

Sophia indicated she would accept a couple of

slices as well. Once the server had carved them and deftly slid the cuts onto their side plates, she picked up her knife and transferred a piece to her dinner plate, slicing through her meat without looking up. Placing the bite in her mouth, she let the buttery tenderness melt on her tongue.

Lucas's eyes widened as he bit into his own meat, and she could practically hear his taste buds cheering.

Unable to hold back a smile, she said, "Good, isn't it? No one does grilled meat like Brazilians." Maybe that sounded a little arrogant, but it was true.

He swallowed, brows lifting. "Seems you've been holding out on me, Sophia."

"Are you complaining about my cooking?"

"Your cooking is…delicious."

Another server arrived just in time to stop the blush she could feel hovering on the edges of her face.

"Are those what I think they are?" he asked, staring at the thinner skewer, which was laden with chicken hearts.

"Yes. They're really good." She nodded to the waiter, who slid three of the grilled hearts onto her plate.

"I think I'll pass." He thanked the waiter but declined. "Besides, I'll get more enjoyment from watching you eat them."

There were times Sophia could almost believe he was Brazilian despite his accent, but there were other moments when it was obvious his link with his homeland had been severed—or at least worn to a hair-thin thread. It made her sad. It also made her aware that playing word games with someone like him was very dangerous, no matter how much fun it seemed at the time.

"Maybe you should try something before you dismiss it out of hand. I bet Marcos is eating all sorts of American foods." She cut off a tiny portion of one of the hearts.

His mouth tightened. "I bet he is. He's probably devouring everything in sight."

Shock flashed through her system. She'd caught hints of anger from time to time in Lucas's attitude when he talked about his brother, but it made no sense. "You make him sound like a bad person. He's not, you know."

He sat back. "I know he's not."

"Then why do you seem to—?"

"He had to take care of me constantly when we were kids." He shrugged. "I'm sure it was a huge relief once I was gone, and he didn't need to worry about me any more. He didn't have to give up his shoes, his food, his blankets. His *life*. My adoption was the best thing that could have happened to him."

She stared at him. Was that really what he thought? That Marcos had viewed him as some kind of burden? Tears pricked at her eyes. "Lucas, your brother grieved terribly when you went away. He already blamed himself for your father's death, and then when you left, he…well, he didn't speak to anyone for months. He kept that picture—the one that's on his television stand—under his pillow and refused to let anyone near it. One of the cafeteria workers heard about it and bought a frame with her own money. Marcos has never taken the picture out of it as far as I know."

"I just assumed he'd be…" He dragged a hand through his hair.

"Well, you were wrong. About him. Maybe even about Brazil."

Forcing herself to take a deep breath, she picked up the fork with the chicken heart and held it out to him. "You were born here, Lucas. I know it may not feel like you belong, but you have this country's blood flowing through your veins. Give it a chance."

From the set of his jaw she wondered if he was going to refuse, but then he took the fork from her and put the piece of meat in his mouth. He chewed. Swallowed.

He handed the fork back and gave her a half-smile. "Different. Not bad. Certainly not what I expected. And thank you for what you said. About Marcos. Someone told me he has a free clinic in one of the *favelas*. Any chance I could see it?"

"Of course. I go down there with him all the time, I'm sure he'd be happy for you to visit. I'll set it up." She paused. "You need to talk to him, Lucas. Tell him what you told me."

"Maybe. Someday."

A gentle sizzle went up her spine at his words. He hadn't dismissed her suggestion out of hand. And he'd grudgingly said the chicken heart wasn't bad, it was just different. He even wanted to venture into the *favela*. Maybe she was wrong. Maybe that link hadn't been sliced completely through after all.

When he reached across the table and picked up her hand, she tilted her head in question.

"There was a little girl at the doctor's office today who looked like you."

"There was?"

He nodded. "She was about four years old. Beautiful, with these huge brown eyes that seemed to see right through you. Just like you did when..." He paused, frowning, his hand tightening around hers.

Sophia's heart picked up speed, thudding louder and louder until she was sure the whole restaurant could hear it. "Like I did when what?"

"When you looked at me in the orphanage." His eyes came up and speared hers. "I just had a quick flash of your face go through my head. Did you meet my brother and me at the orphanage that first day?"

She licked her lips, then nodded.

"You held Marcos's hand but not mine." His voice was soft, as if he was lost in some distant memory. "In fact, after that first glance you acted like I didn't exist."

Only because he'd frightened her. He'd been... too perfect. But then she'd let her guard down and included him into her world, and soon the three of them had done everything together. At least until Lucas had left. Then had come the pain.

And if she wasn't careful, if she let her guard down again, history would repeat itself because he wasn't likely to stay this time, either. "We were all pretty close, from what I remember."

She flicked the little sign to green, unwilling to continue down this path. "I still need to finish packing. Are you ready for the grilled pineapple? It's what we normally finish the meal with."

His lips tightened. "Yes. I know you're anxious to get back to your place."

If he only knew how wrong he was. She just needed to get away from him, because she was so close to giving in to the little kernel of need that was quivering inside her, getting ready to burst open at any second like a piece of popcorn bombarded by microwaves.

Lucas might as well be giving off tons of the stuff, because she felt warm and fidgety whenever he was around. And she had no idea how to make it stop, other than to just remove herself from the vicinity.

Fifteen minutes later they walked out of the restaurant. Sophia handed her parking ticket to the attendant outside, who radioed the number to someone else. Lucas's fingers curled around hers. "Thanks for all you did for me this week. I couldn't have done it without you."

"I think you'd have found a way. I didn't do all that much."

Other than let him kiss her. Undoing his pants as he'd slept. Getting an eyeful the next morning.

And hearing him say a little girl looked like her.

He'd called her beautiful. Twice now. It spun her heart round and round in her chest. "I'm glad I was there."

"I'm glad you were, too." The hand holding hers exerted slight pressure, turning her towards him. "Are you sure you have to—?"

"*Moça?* Your car is here."

The voice to her right made her tense. Before she could pull her hand free and give the man a tip, Lucas beat her to it, pressing a bill into the man's palm with his free hand. *"Obrigado."*

He then walked her round her car and opened her door, only releasing her when she slid into her seat. Going to the other side, he climbed in beside her.

Despite the lunch-hour traffic, they made it back to Marcos's apartment within fifteen minutes, and she punched the button on the box out front, waiting until the entry gate slid open. She then found the apartment's assigned parking space and pulled her little car into it. "Speaking of Marcos, have you heard from him in the last couple of days?"

"No. Although I'm not really expecting him to call. Not after the way he sounded the last time I talked to him."

Yes. He'd sounded in love. Happy.

Sophia was glad for him. But things would have been a whole lot less complicated if he hadn't gone traipsing off to the United States. He'd have been the one dealing with Lucas, not her.

They rode up in the elevator in silence, and the longer it dragged on, the more uncomfortable she got. Surely one of them could come up with a topic of conversation that would fill the next few minutes. Then she'd be packed and on her way. She'd be home in an hour.

Why did that thought not fill her with relief? Once they left the elevator, Lucas took the key out of his pocket and inserted it in the door. The second she passed through it, she started to hurry back to the bedroom, only to stop when she heard her name.

She turned toward him. "Yes?"

"Don't leave without saying goodbye."

She blinked in surprise. Why did those words

have a ring of finality to them? It wasn't like either of them was leaving the country. Oh, yes, of course. Lucas *was* leaving, as soon as he got the all-clear from the doctor. "I won't."

Going into her room and shutting the door, she sank onto the bed and stared at her suitcase. She did not want to toss her things into it and walk away from him.

You're not walking away. You're driving. And you'll only be fifteen minutes away from him in case of an emergency. Besides, this was your idea.

She might as well have been going two thousand miles, though, because once she moved out nothing would be the same.

The same as what, exactly?

No more intimacy like they'd had on the couch. She'd been so close to stretching out beside him and sleeping next to him that night. It had only been the fear of damaging the stitches in his side that had made her go back to her room.

It scared her how right it had felt to kiss him. To crawl onto his lap and want to devour him whole.

Not a smart move, unless she was willing to settle for a short fling.

Grimacing, she got off the bed and picked up

the nearest item of clothing, tossing it into the suitcase. Then another…and another.

Who cared if everything had a million wrinkles? They'd just match the rest of her. On the outside she was bright and bubbly, full of optimism towards life. But inside it was a different story. She had trouble forming attachments with other people. Long-term relationships were next to impossible. Because of her parents? Maybe.

Not even the two men who'd been her lovers once she reached adulthood had scratched beneath the surface. She'd liked them well enough, and sex had been pleasant but it hadn't gone beyond that. Neither of them had stuck around for very long. Marcos was her only lasting friendship.

Which was why Lucas scared her so much. She'd never experienced anything like that molten kiss on the couch. It had taken her by storm, transforming into a dangerous, churning vortex that threatened to suck her into its depths. Besides, he hadn't even tried to talk her out of leaving.

And if he did?

Swallowing, she latched one side of her overnight case before realizing she'd left her straightening iron in the other room. Opening the door carefully, she eased into the hallway and scurried for the bathroom, hoping she didn't run into him on the way. As soon as she got that last item packed she was out of there.

Lucas was in the living room, pouring himself a stiff drink, when he heard a noise behind him. A throat clearing.

Forcing himself not to spin around, he set the decanter back on the tray at the bar and capped it. He lifted the glass and took a healthy swallow of the fiery liquid before finally turning to face her.

"Are you off?"

"Yes." She licked her bottom lip, curling it in slightly as her teeth came down to meet it, drawing his attention to them. "You asked me not to leave without saying goodbye."

He took another drink, and the burn of the liquid washed across his epiglottis then flowed into his stomach a few seconds later. "So say it."

"I'm sorry?"

What was wrong with him? It wasn't like she was walking away from a twenty-year marriage, so why was there a part inside him that was taking this personally? Acting like she couldn't stand to be around him?

He moved towards her, hearing her rough intake of breath as he did. Instead of stepping back, though, she held her ground, her chin lifting in order to continue meeting his gaze.

Lowering his voice, his fingers clenched the drink. "Say goodbye."

He waited for the word, expecting her to hurl it at him and then turn on her heel and walk away. Instead, she watched him as if trying to figure something out.

Unable to help himself, he reached up and touched the side of his whiskey glass to her jaw, dragging it slowly down the length of it until it rested on the delicate point of her chin. Her lips parted and he brushed the rim of the glass across her top lip and then the full bottom one, using the slightest pressure to open her mouth even further.

She still made no move to leave.

He took her hand and lifted it, curling it around the tumbler. "Take a drink."

She hesitated and then obediently tipped it, taking a small sip of liquid, her mouth touching the glass where his had, her throat moving as she swallowed.

A spear of raw desire went through his gut, the point lodging somewhere deep inside him.

There was no way he was going to pull it back out. Not yet.

"Stay one more night. Just one."

The fingers of his injured arm curved around her nape, the movement jarring his shoulder, but he ignored the pain, wanting nothing more than to banish the fantasies he'd had about her once and for all.

He only knew one way to do that. Experience them for real. All of them. She'd let him kiss her. Would she let him do more than that?

She licked her lips. "Okay."

Lucas took the whiskey glass from her, tossing the rest of its contents down his throat before letting the tumbler drop to the thick area rug beneath his feet and leaving it there.

The last time he'd kissed her he'd fallen asleep. Well, this time, even if he wound up flat on his back, there was no way his eyes were shutting—not even to blink. Not until he'd drunk as deeply of Sophia as he had of that whiskey. Not until her heat washed over him and through him, obliterating every other thought.

Then, and only then, would he let her go.

CHAPTER TWELVE

A FEW MINUTES ago she'd wondered what she'd do if he asked her not to leave. Well, now she knew.

Sophia ignored the glass he'd dropped a second ago, unable to look away from his smoldering gaze.

Warm hands came up and cupped her face. "I want you in this house. In my bedroom."

"Why?" She wasn't sure where the question had come from, but once it was out there it was too late to retract it. Why couldn't she simply accept that he wanted her? Even if it was just for a single night?

His eyes narrowed slightly. "Do either of us need a reason?"

Okay, that stung a bit, but not enough to make her back away, maybe because her knees were jelly at this point. "I guess not."

Maybe he sensed something in her voice, because his thumbs brushed over her cheekbones. "Sophia, if you haven't been able to tell how much

I want you—have wanted you since I first laid eyes on you—then I've been hiding it better than I thought."

Since he'd first laid eyes on her. Those words sent a shiver rippling through her.

Because, like him, she'd wanted this for quite some time…probably more than she should have.

With that, she closed the gap between them and stood on tiptoe until her lips connected with his.

Lucas went totally still for a heartbeat or two, and she wondered if he might change his mind. Then, with a low groan, his hands tunneled deep into her hair as he stepped into the kiss, head turning sideways, mouth opening to fully take hers in a searing kiss.

Her neck arched beneath the force of it, but his palm was right there at the back of her head, supporting her, allowing him to move against her mouth as hard and as fast as he wanted.

And, *Deus*, she wanted it, too.

His arms were blocking her from reaching his shoulders, so she settled for wrapping her fingers around his forearms, needing desperately to hold onto something as his tongue entered her mouth in one rough thrust that took her breath away.

It was as if he'd finally thrown off the chains

of control, and what it awoke within her was almost primal. Sophia's hips connected with his as she moved between his splayed legs, feeling him hard against her belly.

Her heels were high, but not high enough.

Stilettos.

The thought flashed through her head. She should have worn her highest heels, because she wanted that pressure lower.

As if reading her mind, his knees bent, one hand going to her butt and cupping it as his erection found the bone of her pelvis and pressed hard.

Oh! So close. So very close.

But still not quite there.

His fingers trailed down the back of her skirt until he reached the crook of her knee, wrapping tight around it. The pressure made her mouth water.

Then with one decisive tug her inner thigh slid up, tender flesh scraping along the hard muscles of his leg.

His mouth left hers, lips trailing over her cheekbone until he reached her ear. "Keep your leg right there. Don't move."

No. No moving. Check.

Her breath hissed in when his body gave a subtle

shift that had his leg between hers, moving deeper until his thigh rested right where she needed him the most. *Yes!* The hand that had been supporting her knee abandoned it, his arm wrapping around her lower back instead as he hauled her fully against him.

He held perfectly still, his breath rasping against her ear as he suddenly contracted and released the muscles of his thigh in just that spot.

Deus!

He repeated the act. This time a moan worked its way up from her throat.

"Shh, Sophia…just feel."

She bit her lips as she held herself still and silent as he tensed against her over and over.

The experience was incredible, as if they, along with the world around them, had frozen in time, leaving only the rhythmic flick-flick of his flesh against hers. A light switch turning on-off…on-off. Her universe shrank down to that one tiny point on her body as she anticipated each sweet surge of energy just before it hit.

It was relentless. Her elevated thigh trembled against his leg, but she didn't move. Couldn't. Didn't dare.

Tighten. Release. Tighten… With each change

a crank turned somewhere inside her and a spring wound tighter and tighter.

Her eyes fluttered shut, trying to combat the growing tension.

Too soon. Not yet.

Lucas's breathing changed, grew harsher, and she realized his erection was pressed hard against the curve of her hip.

Seeking release just as badly as she was.

He wanted her. Needed her. Now.

Like a flare going off inside her, she ignited, the force of the blast surging up and through her body, gaining momentum until the shock wave hit her vocal cords. Holding back was no longer an option. She cried out, clutching at his shoulders for all she was worth as wave after wave of pleasure spun her round and round like a loosed top.

Lucas's guttural groan of encouragement met her ear about the time his mouth clamped over hers, kissing her in a fury, absorbing all the nonsensical sounds she continued to make, his teeth and tongue echoing everything she was feeling.

Oh, God...oh, God...oh, God.

He gripped the back of her knee, maybe realizing she was in very real danger of collapsing to the floor in a heap, then gently allowed her foot to slide back to the floor before wrapping both arms around her. He lifted his head, murmuring to her as the dizzying rotation slowed, along with her racing heart.

The humiliating realization hit her. He'd barely touched her. Had simply flexed his muscles—literally—and sent her into the stratosphere.

"I… You…" She tried to find the words to say, but nothing was as it should be.

He nuzzled her cheek, totally unaware of the conflict raging within her. "*I* am not done yet. Not by a long shot. Neither are you. That was just the appetizer."

"It was?"

He moved to her ear, his teeth nipping her lobe, sending a shiver through her. "I told you when this day came it wouldn't be on a metal table, and it wouldn't be done in a rush." He chuckled. "This was the only way I could keep the last part of that promise. If I'd have been inside you a second ago, it would have been all over. And the last thing I want is for…*this* to be over."

Anticipation slid through her veins, his growled words erasing her doubts. He didn't think she was too eager. He'd *wanted* her to climax—had intended to push her over the edge. Because he hadn't been able to trust himself not to join her.

She reached up and wrapped her arms around his neck, suddenly very glad it wasn't over either. Her bravado came back, at least a tiny portion of it. "So if it's not going to be on a metal table, then what kind of table did you have in mind? Wooden?" Her glance went to the dining room where the huge mahogany table stretched long and wide.

"Uh-uh." A hungry gleam came to his eyes. "Not this time."

There was going to be a next time?

Why not? Right now she'd give him just about anything. Including as many "next times" as he wanted.

He went on. "I don't want you sliding away from me. I want you sliding *on* me. All the way down. Just like I imagined it."

Her heart stuttered. The man's words painted a picture that was all too clear. And that was one portrait she wanted to be in. Right now.

"My room," she whispered.

"Mine." His palms slid down her arms until he'd captured her hands. "If I could pick you up, there'd be no doubt where you'd end up. Or who'd be on top. I'd like nothing better than to feel you sink deep into the mattress, just before I sink deep into you."

Meu Deus do céu.

Still gripping her by one wrist, he towed her into Marcos's bedroom, not bothering to close the door behind him. Why should he? No one was home.

No interruptions.

The third part of his promise.

Her nipples tightened, breasts aching. He was right. He couldn't be on top because of his side and shoulder, so she'd be doing most of the work. That was absolutely fine by her. As inexperienced as she was in the art of seduction—and she was just beginning to realize how shallow her previous wading pools had been—she could probably figure out what went where and when. But since she was evidently heading this thing up, maybe she should be allowed to call a few of the shots.

She reached out and gripped a handful of his T-shirt with her free hand just before he reached the bed, stopping him. When he turned towards her with a concerned frown, she smiled. "Don't worry, Lucas. You're going to get your fun. But it's my turn now."

With that she tugged free of his grip on her wrist.

One brow went up. "I think you've had your turn," he pointed out.

She laughed, knowing exactly what he was referring to. "That's where you're wrong. You liked seeing me like that, making me lose control. That was all about you. This part is for me."

With that she slid her hands under his T-shirt, allowing her thumbs to snag on the hem and avoiding his injured side, while inching the fabric up his torso and smoothing her palms over the warmth of his skin.

His breath hissed in. "This is not my idea of fun."

"Sure it is." Wow, maybe he was right. Being uninhibited had its good points. The nubs of masculine nipples passed beneath her fingertips, and she paused. "Lift your arms."

"Sophia." The warning tone didn't deter her one bit.

"I'm just taking your shirt off. I've done it before, remember?"

He did as she asked, and she tugged the piece of clothing over his head. Once it was on the floor, she reached up and kissed the lower part of his jaw, loving the way the stubble felt on her lips, shivering as she remembered the way it had scraped her tender flesh as he'd slid his cheek along hers in the living room.

His hand came up and tangled in her hair, but when he directed her towards his mouth and started to lean down, she pressed her lips to his shoulder instead, inching her way down his body. The pounding of his heart beneath his chest wall met her open mouth at one point, inciting her to continue her quest.

"Sophia…" This time her name was a whispered plea.

She reached the nipple she'd touched a moment earlier and flicked her tongue across it. His breath shuddered in on a strangled groan. When she closed around the tight flesh, his reaction was instantaneous, his hand tightening in her hair. She thought for a moment he was going to drag her away from him, but then he bit out a low curse and pressed her closer instead.

Need spurted through her, and she suddenly knew exactly how Lucas had felt as he'd sent her into oblivion a few minutes ago. His obvious pleasure fueled her own, a vicious cycle that was anything but vicious.

Moving to his other nipple, she hoped to distract him long enough to…

There.

She found the button to his pants and managed to slide it free. Her fingers went to the tab, this time knowing full well what lay beneath it.

Maybe they wouldn't make it to the bed at all. Maybe she'd simply wind her leg around him the way she'd done in the living room and take him that way.

Zi-i-i-p. The most beautiful sound in the world.

Lucas tried to take a step back, but she followed him, her lips never leaving their chosen spot, her fingers squeezing between the edges of his pants and finding him hard and ready. She applied more suction, hoping he could feel it all the way down there, like she had during that last violent kiss.

On cue, his erection jumped beneath her hand. *Oh, yes.* This was definitely her idea of fun.

She'd never known what a huge turn-on it was to have a man stand there while you were free to roam his body…explore every inch of him.

And she meant to do exactly that. With her mouth.

Decision made, she ran her tongue down the warm flesh of his chest, continuing down his stomach, feeling the bump, bump, bump as she cruised down his abdomen, like three speed bumps that warned her to slow down...warned her of danger ahead.

What if she liked danger?

Because she certainly liked what was ahead.

She tugged his briefs down over his swollen flesh, baring him to her eyes.

Almost there.

She sank to her knees and opened her mouth wide, just as a gurgled sound came from above her. The hand still embedded in her hair tugged sharply enough to get her attention.

"No." He dragged her back upright. "If this is going to end, that's not where I want to finish it." Power-walking backwards to the bed, he sat on it, looking hotter than she'd imagined possible with his fly open and his penis straining above the black elastic of his underwear.

"Take off your clothes," he murmured. "Starting with your blouse."

The woman had almost made him come, and she'd barely even touched him. Just a couple of squeezes with her fingers, and he'd been almost there. Then, seeing those red lips part, wet and round, as she'd got ready to go down on him had sent lust crashing through his skull. He'd wanted her to do it, had started to close his eyes in ecstasy, but what he'd told her was the truth.

He wanted to sink into her depths and wonder if he was going to survive the experience. And he wanted that to happen with her sitting on top of him, where he could see every nuance of that expressive face as he brought her to another peak. And he would. Whatever it took to hold off his demons until then, he'd do.

Sex had never been a clawing, rabid creature that strained to break free. Until today.

Even as the thought came and went, her fingers skated down the length of her silky, bronze-colored top, flicking open one button after another. She tugged it free of the waistband of her narrow black skirt until she revealed a lacy bra— red.

Fire-engine red, five-alarm red.

It looked as hot as he felt.

He swallowed as the blouse dropped to the floor.

When she reached behind her back, he stopped her. "Come here."

She licked her lips and hesitated, so he repeated

the command, his voice lowering to coax her forward. "Sophia, come here."

She moved towards him, and when she was within reach he slid his hands behind her back, relishing the soft, smooth skin beneath his fingers. He tugged her a few steps closer. The bed was high, the perfect height for all kinds of things. Had Marcos bought it with this type of encounter in mind?

Screw Marcos. He had nothing to do with this.

But the bed made him change his mind. Having Sophia sitting on top of him wasn't how this was going to play out. Not with the precarious state he was in. He needed to be in control of how fast, how deep, or he was done for.

He leaned forward and inhaled the intoxicating scent coming off her skin, her arousal hitting his system like nothing he'd ever experienced. His nose swept to the side, grazing the pucker of the rosy nipple just visible through the wispy lace fabric.

"Lucas, please." She braced her hands on his shoulders and tried to ease him back on the bed.

"Uh-uh. My turn," he reminded her. It felt so good to say that, felt wonderful to have her body right here where he could touch, taste, see every tiny mark, lick across anything he wanted to. As if to demonstrate, he pressed the tip of his tongue to the underside of the nipple in front of him, pushing up, then flicking across it.

She moaned, fingers tightening on his shoulders and pressing closer.

Yes. He liked to make her do that. Hoped to make her do a whole lot more.

His fingers crept under her skirt, walking slowly up the backs of her thighs until he found the lower edge of her panties, following the line around. He swallowed at the moist heat coming from her center, knew exactly how it would feel to drive home. And he wanted to. Ached to. Needed to.

He dragged her underwear down her legs as he continued to lap over her nipple with broad, firm strokes, the tip so very hard against his lips, his tongue.

"Step out."

As soon as she did so, she started to hike up her skirt and climb onto the bed, but he stopped her. Standing to his feet, he ignored her soft, disappointed murmur. Not much longer. But he needed a condom. Hoped his brother at least had something in one of these drawers. But, first, one more thing.

He moved behind her and planted his hand between her shoulder blades, his thumb rubbing back and forth with sweeping strokes. "Bend over the bed for me."

She glanced back at him in confusion.

"Like this," he said, applying easy pressure with his palm and watching as she bent to his will, just as he'd bent to hers earlier.

And, yes, it was so very good. But it was about to get better. "Stay there, Sophia. Just for a minute."

She whimpered, sounding as turned on as he felt. He shed the rest of his clothing and yanked open a drawer or two.

A blue box winked up at him. Success!

Tearing open the first packet he could get his hands on and dropping the box on the floor, he sheathed himself then moved behind her, inching her skirt up the backs of her thighs, until she stood exposed. Her heels just added to the sensual image.

He leaned over her, positioning himself against her slick heat, gripping her hips, his legs trembling with the effort of holding back. "Ready?"

"Yes." Her butt inched higher, a glorious, beautiful offering. One he could resist no longer.

He entered her in one quick thrust, hearing the wind rush from her lungs as her body sank into the plush surface of the mattress. Forcing himself to suck down a couple of deep breaths when all he wanted to do was pump like a wild man, he put his mouth to her ear. "Are you okay?"

"Mmm. Yes." She pushed back against him, her hips rotating as if trying to force him to move.

He wanted to. Hell, he wasn't sure he could avoid it. But he desperately wanted her to go with him.

Letting go of one of her hips, he pushed his hand between her body and the mattress, sliding it down the softness of her belly until he reached the narrow strip of hair between her legs.

Damn, he'd thought the heat coming off her panties was hot. That had been nothing compared to this. She was a furnace, searing him inside and out.

He touched the spot he knew would do the most good then angled his hips and began moving in short, controlled bursts.

She matched his tempo, burying her face in the mattress, her hands clenching and unclenching the coverlet as she panted, trying to force him to go deeper. She was close, her legs widening to give him better access. Access that he immediately took advantage of as he continued to use his body and fingers, fighting his own release every step of the way. She was gorgeous, the long length of her spine stretched over the bed, the swell of her hips moving back and forth to the rhythm he'd chosen.

"Oh! Oh!" Her body stiffened, and like a jockey approaching the finish line he leaned forward, urging her on even as his own adrenaline shot through his veins. It hit, her and then him, the strong contractions of her body causing him to crest almost immediately. Her fierce moan ripped through him, as everything turned inside out and he pressed his face to the side of her neck as he rode both of their climaxes out to the very end.

He slowed, the muscles in his legs trembling as he tried not to rest all his weight on her, not that his injured side would allow him to collapse fully on top of her.

His hands followed her arms until he reached her fingers, then threaded his own through them. He kissed the side of her neck, allowing his eyes to close as he tried to slow his breathing and regain his sense of the here and now.

Here: his brother's bedroom…his brother's condom…his brother's friend.

Now: probably the biggest mistake of his life…
and there was absolutely no way to fix it.

As his sweat began to dry to a sticky film, reality crept in, its sharp talons tearing through the
ecstasy he'd felt seconds earlier and revealing the
sinister truth hidden behind the haze of lust.

What the hell?

He'd just had the best sex of his whole damn
life, so what was he doing, overanalyzing everything?

He didn't believe in steady relationships, but
that's not what this was. It was simply a one-time
event that was anything but simple. It would probably never happen again.

Something he was already regretting.

But how could he ask for more of the same?
How could he tell a woman whose parents had
thrown her away that he only wanted her for a
little while—that when he was through, he'd do
exactly what they'd done and leave her behind
without a second glance?

CHAPTER THIRTEEN

DID HE WANT a next time or didn't he?

Sophia stood beside the bed, her blouse hanging off one shoulder. She'd jerked awake in shock this morning as she'd realized where she was. What she'd done. Each and every second of their time together replayed through her head.

She'd scooted out of bed, intent on getting away as fast as possible. Why was she still here? She could be already out of here.

Just through the doorway lay her overnight bag, and freedom. She tugged her shirt over her shoulder, and did up a couple of the buttons before she stopped again.

Leaving would be the smart thing.

Which was why she'd slept with him in the first place, right? Because it had been smart?

Deus. It might not have been wise, but it had been good. Really good. Better than anything she'd done in her entire life.

She'd always played it safe—safe job, safe

friends…safe men. She'd never really explored her sensual side. Not that she'd even thought she had much of one, until now.

Who would even know? Not Marcos. He was in the States. And Lucas was only here for another week or two at the most, so there wasn't much chance that he'd blab to anyone, right?

Her legs trembled just thinking about the possibilities. She smoothed her skirt down over her thighs, realizing something was missing.

Her panties! *Deus*, she'd almost forgotten he'd taken them off, leaving her skirt on. Her glance skated around the edge of the bed, expecting to see them lying on the floor. She could put off making a firm decision until she found them.

That was if she could get up the courage to ask him straight out if he wanted her to stay for a few more days. Once he was gone, life could go back to normal. But until then she could live on the wild side. Be uninhibited. Just like Lucas was.

Look for the panties then *think!*

A spilled box of condoms reminded her in all too graphic terms what had happened here last night.

When he'd bent her over that bed…

She closed her eyes and took a deep breath as a wave of lust crashed over her. Then another.

"Where are you going?"

The low question made her jump, her eyelids coming apart in a flash and turning her into a chicken. "I was just getting ready to take a shower before, um, going home."

So much for asking him about a repeat performance.

Lucas sat up, still naked and sporting a morning erection that made all kinds of crazy thoughts whisk through her head. Like crawling back into bed and running her fingers through that gloriously mussed hair until he begged for mercy. Then she'd finish him off.

"What's the rush?" he said. "We can have breakfast and talk about last night."

Talk. Okay, she'd definitely not thought this through very well. She'd been counting on action to carry the day. Besides, if he wanted her to stay, he'd say something. Like he had last night.

She gave a little wave of her hand. "Last night was great. We've both been under a lot of pressure recently. And pressure eventually needs to find an outlet. A pressure valve. Sex is a known stress reliever. *I* certainly feel better, how about you?"

Wow, that was brilliant. It even sounded pretty believable, considering the words had tumbled out at around a hundred miles per hour.

Smooth, Sophia, very smooth.

"A pressure valve." His eyes narrowed, and he swung his legs over the side of the bed, still making no effort to cover himself. "That's what this was?"

She concentrated on her panties. If Lucas wanted her to leave, she really should take them with her. After all, what if Marcos came home and found them? She tilted her head sideways and tried to see past the line of darkness beneath the bed. Her underwear was red, the carpet white, how hard could it be to spot them?

"I think so." Her voice was still pretty steady, even though her heart was pounding at an alarming rate. "We're practically strangers, so how could it be anything else?"

Wow, maybe she was more sophisticated than she'd thought.

Instead of smiling with relief, the edges of his mouth tightened, turning white. "You make a habit of having sex with strangers?"

Oops. Something had just zigged when it should have zagged. "No, of course not."

"Just with me. A stranger."

Yikes.

"Well, it was just one night and…" She shrugged. Forced her eyes to keep scanning the floor for her errant underwear. She was tempted to go down on her hands and knees and peer under the bed, except she didn't have any panties on, and he was still so…so *up*.

"So if it was *more* than one night, that would make us…what, exactly?"

More than one night?

Her head came up, and she stared at him. "Are you asking me to stay longer? And do more of what we did last night?"

Before she realized what he was going to do, he'd snagged her wrist and tugged her between his splayed legs. Warm hands went to the backs of her knees and began gliding upwards.

"I was going to discuss this over breakfast, but the answer is yes to both questions. I want you to stay. And I want to do more of what we did last night. Much more." His slow smile burned away any last doubt she might have harbored. "But first I want to make one thing perfectly clear."

"Wh-what's that?" she squeaked, her heart rate already spiking into the hundreds.

Using the hand that lay just below the bare flesh of her butt to hold her in place, he reached beneath his pillow and pulled out her panties, letting them dangle precariously off one finger. "You and I, Sophia, are *anything* but strangers."

"So this is it?"

After a few suspicious glances and one confrontation they stood in the heart of the *favela* where a red-bricked shack lay deserted—no sign to indicate it was a clinic. Sophia had needed to reassure a couple of men who'd blocked their path that they meant no harm. Luckily they knew her— they just didn't know him. The second she'd told them Lucas was Marcos's brother, they'd stood aside. Word had traveled fast, because people came out of their homes, a few of them waving.

"Yes. This is it."

Sophia adjusted her dark tank top, glancing down as if to make sure the small red mark he'd left on her right breast this morning wasn't showing. It wasn't, but she'd know it was there…would serve as a reminder of what they'd done. When he'd awoken to find her eyes on him, her shirt hanging open to reveal the entire right cup of her lacy red bra, he'd wanted her all over again. Then she'd mentioned home...had called him a stranger, and anger had spurted through his system. He'd needed to show her exactly how well he knew her. Starting with the silky flesh beneath that bra. The way she'd squirmed, moaning as he'd sucked her flesh into his mouth, lapped over it with his tongue afterwards, had driven him crazy.

His body had reacted all over again.

So his brother wasn't a stranger to her. But *he* was?

Not the time, Carvalho.

Sophia put a key into the lock on a door that looked like it could be kicked in by a small child. Pushing it open as far as it would go, she flipped a cardboard sign on the inside of the door so that it read *Aberto*, then motioned him inside.

It could have been the setting of any one of his charity trips, but this was his home country, and from what he could remember, this was *his* favela. A dirt floor made of the ubiquitous red clay that covered much of Sao Paulo was clean swept and the unpainted walls were raw bricks of the same color. A clay tile roof topped it off. Maybe the colors had been chosen to match the ground. Everything had the same muddy red tones.

He glanced around. "Where are your supplies?"

Sophia nodded at a folding table propped against one wall and two white plastic chairs next to it. "That's it. We don't leave medicines here. Keeping anything of value invites a break-in."

She went over to the table and turned it on its side, opening and locking the legs in place.

"Here, let me help."

"No need. I can do it."

He started to insist then bit back the words. Forcing her to accept his help was what Marcos would have done. And Lucas had strived his whole life to never make anyone feel as guilty and suffocated as he had while under his brother's watchful care.

But Sophia had said his brother hadn't resented doing any of the things he remembered him doing.

Instead, Marcos had grieved.

Maybe she was right. He should talk to him once he got back.

He glanced at the sign on the door. "Are we seeing patients today?"

"Might as well now that we're here, don't you think?" Her movements seemed quick. Jerky. She adjusted her shirt again. Maybe she wasn't as okay with this whole setup as he'd thought.

He caught her arm. "Hey. Stop for a second."

Looking into her eyes, he tried to read behind the warm brown irises. "Are you okay with staying at the house?"

"By the house, you mean your room, I'm assuming?"

Okay, he wasn't going to get into the fact that it wasn't actually his room. "Yes. Are you having second thoughts?"

"After this morning? Hardly."

Relief swept over him, just as there was the sound of a throat clearing from the doorway. Lucas let go of her and turned to find an elderly man with a young child standing there. The man eyed him, then turned to Sophia. *"Onde está Dr. Pinheiro?"*

She smiled at the newcomer. "You know Marcos doesn't like to be called that, Senhor Silvano, especially by someone who knew his father. And he's traveling right now." Sweeping a hand in Lucas's direction, she went on. "This is his brother, Lucas. He's a doctor, too."

Old wizened brows crept toward the heavens. "Lucas? Little Lucas Pinheiro?"

He stiffened at the name. "It's Lucas Carvalho now but, yes, I'm Marcos's brother."

The little girl headed for Sophia, who swept her

into her arms, planting a kiss on her dusty cheek. "How's my little angel today?"

"Fine."

Sophia carried the child to the other side of the room, in a not-so-subtle attempt to give Lucas and the old man some privacy.

"You've never been here before," the man said.

Actually, he had. Just in time to be shot by a couple of thugs who evidently lived somewhere in the *favela*. But he wasn't about to say it. "No, sir. I live in the States."

He noted that the man kept one hand hidden behind his back, and a sick thumping set to work inside Lucas's head.

It wasn't a gun.

He decided to tackle the obvious. "What can I help you with?"

The man pursed his lips, studying him for a moment. "You think you can pull a meat fork out of my back without breaking it—or killin' me? Wife wouldn't like it if I ruined it."

What? The man had a heavy accent and there were more teeth missing than present, but surely he hadn't just said… "Could you repeat that?"

"A fork, son. I have a fork stuck in my back." He proceeded to shuffle his feet to the left, turning his body. Lo and behold, the glint of twin metal tines topped with a wooden handle appeared from beneath the man's thin button-up shirt, along with a large red stain.

Lucas moved closer immediately. "How did this happen?"

The man gave an embarrassed shrug. "I didn't like the wife's dinner. She didn't like me saying so."

Holy hell!

"She stabbed you with a meat fork?"

He chuckled and glanced over his shoulder. "Actually, she was all worked up, and I backed away from her as quickly as I could. The sink was full of dishes. If I didn't know better, I'd think she planted it there on purpose. Good thing the clinic opened up or I'd have had to ask her to pull it out. And with the mood she's in…well, I'd rather not take any chances."

Lucas could honestly say he'd never pulled a fork out of a man's back. Ever. Luckily, the tines weren't terribly long, and it looked like they'd just hit the fleshy part on his side. But he might need a tetanus shot, if he wasn't current.

"Soph? Do you think you could keep your little friend occupied for a while?"

"Why?" She turned his way, eyes widening as she saw the problem. "Oh. Um, yes. We'll just go outside for a short walk. Call if you need me."

As she started to scoot past him, he caught a quick glimpse of red where her tank top had slipped to reveal a sliver of her current bra of choice.

Hmm. Red must be her favorite color. That was okay, it was quickly becoming his favorite as well. He couldn't hold back a smile as he turned to the task of righting Mr. Silvano's wrong.

When it came down to it, whether it involved sharp forks or bright red bras, men were pretty much at the mercy of the fairer sex. And the weapons they wielded could be downright lethal.

CHAPTER FOURTEEN

"PRECISO AJUDA!"

The cry for help came at the same time as the alarm on a heart-rate monitor went off down the hallway. Sophia jumped from her station as Sonia, Sílvio Airton's daughter, came skidding out of the room at the end of the corridor, waving to her.

Oh, no! Sílvio had improved enough that he was scheduled to go home later this morning. She'd just been writing up his discharge papers.

Hurrying down the corridor and entering his room, she took one look at the monitor and saw the classic wiggly line that signaled V-fib, a potentially fatal arrhythmia.

Jesse, her swollen belly showing she hadn't yet given birth, stood close by, her hand over her mouth, tears spilling down her cheeks.

Deus!

Sophia urged everyone back, knowing more personnel would arrive within a minute, along with a crash cart. Until then she moved to the head of the bed and quickly assessed her patient. Grabbing a bag valve mask and fitting it over Sílvio's mouth, she squeezed the device at regular intervals, getting off around three pushes of air before another nurse arrived with the crash cart, followed by a third, who asked the frantic relatives to step outside with her. Relief swept over her as she called out orders to other members of the team as they arrived, thankful Sílvio's family wouldn't have to witness the frenzy as the resuscitation attempts swung into full gear. By the time a doctor arrived thirty seconds later, CPR was already in progress.

Come on, Sílvio, fight!

A nurse lubricated the defibrillator paddles and charged them up, handing them over to the doctor when he asked for them.

"Clear!" Everyone stepped back as he pressed the paddles to the patient's chest and activated the trigger. Sílvio's muscles contracted as the charge went through him. Sophia sent up a silent prayer as everyone stopped to look at the cardiac monitor, waiting to see if his heart would restart itself.

"Still in V-fib," she said, stomach tightening.

"Again, charged to three hundred," called the doctor.

The nurse upped the charge of electricity to be delivered and as soon as it reached the desired level, the doctor attempted conversion again. A second of asystole crossed the monitor after the electricity was delivered, and everyone held their breath, hoping the heart's natural pacemaker would reboot itself and send lifesaving blood pumping through the Sílvio's tired body once again.

Instead, the flatline persisted, and Sophia sucked down a quick breath as everyone jumped back to action. Defibrillation was useless against asystole. Sophia intubated him and reattached the bag valve mask, while another nurse began chest compressions.

Forty-five minutes later the room looked like a battleground with used equipment littering every surface. All to no avail.

The doctor shook his head. "Let's call it."

Although she cared for all her patients, there were some who tugged at Sophia's heartstrings no matter how objective she tried to be. Sílvio was one of those patients. Letting go of his bag valve mask and taking a step back made her eyes burn, even though she knew the doctor was right. There was nothing more to be done. His body had just been too tired to keep fighting.

Limbs trembling as the rush of adrenaline began to subside, she concentrated on taking long steadying breaths as the doctor called out the time of death and the recording nurse wrote it on the chart.

Looking down at her patient's weathered face, Sophia hoped that somewhere he knew how hard they'd fought for him. How hard his family had fought for him.

She hoped he knew how much he'd be missed.

Her throat contracted and, unbidden, Lucas's face swam into focus.

Not the time, Sophia.

The team went to work disassembling the equipment as someone went out to inform the family. Sonia and Jesse would want some time alone with him to say their goodbyes, and she wanted the scene to look as peaceful as possible.

She brushed her hand across the thin grey tufts of Sílvio's hair, before removing his intubation tube and gently swabbing his mouth clean.

The doctor, maybe noticing how shaky she was, laid a hand on her shoulder. "We did what we could, Sophia."

She blinked hard. "I know. He didn't even get to hold his grandbaby." That probably didn't make much sense, as the doctor didn't know about any of that. "He was just…nice, you know?"

"Yes, he was." One more squeeze, and he slid out of the room and on to his next patient.

The team filed out one at a time, Sophia being the last to leave. When she finally exited and saw who was waiting at her desk, the burning in her eyes increased.

Lucas stood at the end of the hallway, hands propped low on his hips, looking sexy and alive. Somehow it didn't seem right. Not after what she'd just been through. Her steps slowed as she glanced at the clock, surprised to see that technically she was already off duty.

Damn. She hoped to hell he didn't want to dissect their decision to keep sleeping together, because she just wasn't up to it right now.

Especially as she could almost feel the mark he'd left on her tingling to life.

Because despite the fact that things between them were fun and the sex was out of this world, she realized that when it came time for Lucas to go, she was going to miss him. And she didn't *want* to miss him. Wanted things to remain light and uncomplicated.

Could anything really remain uncomplicated with this man? He was complex and impossible to understand…and, God, she was glad he was there.

Pulling even with him, she tilted her head to look at him. Eyes swimming with sympathy, he gazed back at her. "I'm sorry about your patient."

"You heard." She wasn't surprised. News traveled like wildfire on the ward. Then again, with Sonia and Jesse standing in the hallway, their fear and anguish obvious, it wasn't hard to realize what was going on in that room.

"I asked someone." He reached out to brush a strand of damp hair off her brow. "Do you want to go somewhere?"

Nothing about their situation. Just an intuitive knowledge that she needed to get away.

She closed her eyes and started to wipe the back of her hand across her brow, only to realize she still had her surgical gloves on. She stared at them for several long seconds. Somehow taking them off seemed so…final.

As if he knew what she was thinking, Lucas took one of her hands and peeled the glove off, and then the other, rolling one into the other like a pair of socks. "Come on. Let me take you somewhere for some coffee or a hot meal."

She nodded, unable to do anything else, still not sure why he was there, but it didn't matter. Signing off her shift and collecting her purse, she murmured goodbye to one of the other nurses. As they walked towards the exit, she was all too aware of the warm, firm hand beneath her elbow. "I parked on the other side of the hospital."

"Leave it. We'll take a taxi."

"Are you sure? They're hideously expensive."

"Less than they are in California. I took one to the hospital today."

She'd dropped him off after their brief run to the *favela*, telling him she'd be back to get him for his therapy session—hadn't stopped to wonder how he'd arrived. "I'm sorry I didn't make it back in time."

"Don't worry about it. I already cancelled today's session."

"But you shouldn't. You need to—"

"Take you someplace quiet. It's not just about your patient. I need to talk to you." Wrapping an arm around her waist, he set her feet back in motion.

Something in her stomach leaped. Talk to her.

About what? "It doesn't have anything to do with…you know what, does it?"

"No. It's about Marcos."

Her stomach squirmed again. "Is he all right? Maggie?"

"I'm assuming they're both fine, as I haven't heard from them." He gave her a smile that was half exasperation, half compassion. "Will you please keep walking? It's nothing bad. I promise."

Nothing bad. Well, that was something.

Fifteen minutes later the cab stopped at Ibirapueira Park in the middle of downtown São Paulo. She glanced at him in surprise. Sophia loved this place, came here whenever she got the chance. Although it was crowded on the weekends, it was a delight during the rest of the week. A green oasis in the middle of a city filled with concrete walls and choking pollution.

"Is this okay? I thought we could get some truck food and find a quiet place in the grass."

She smiled and touched his arm. "This is perfect, Lucas. Thank you so much."

It *was* perfect. Maybe a little too perfect.

They got out of the taxi and strolled into the park, bypassing the bike rental stand and the parking ticket vendor. The air was cool for this time of year, and Sophia sucked it down, the lush green grass and towering trees never failing to instill in her a sense of peace.

She glanced at Lucas who strolled next to her. "Are you sure you're up to this?"

"As long as you don't try any fancy moves, I think I'll be able to keep up."

Her stomach shimmied beneath her ribcage at the memory of just how well he'd been able to keep up last night…and this morning. Hard to believe that less than twelve hours had passed since then.

No, she was the one in danger of not keeping up.

The sensual games Lucas seemed so adept at were all new to her, which was why she'd agreed to his request to stay. She wanted to explore. To learn what her body was capable of. Maybe that's why both of her other relationships had fizzled out after only a few months. Neither of them had elicited the wild passion that Lucas brought to the surface.

They reached a fork in the road, and Lucas paused as if not sure which way to go. That's right. He wasn't familiar with the park. Or his birth culture, for that matter. "Let's go to the right. There's a nice place off the beaten path. We can pick up some food at one of the stands on the way, if you still want to eat."

"Sounds good to me."

Minutes later, Sophia carried several spicy meat kabobs, while Lucas held two chilled green coconuts, the tops removed with a single whack of a machete, leaving a small hole through which to stick a straw. They found a shady spot in the grass, far enough from the pavement that they had a bit of privacy but close enough to watch the daily activity in the park—whether it be runners pounding the pavement or riders rolling by on inline skates or bicycles.

Lucas toed his loafers off, enjoying the freedom that always came with ridding himself of his shoes. He leaned back on one elbow, careful to keep his side fairly straight, and took a sip of the coconut water. Crystal clear and slightly sweet, the icy liquid slid down his throat like a dream.

"Another thing I don't remember." He studied the fruit. "Although I'm sure I must have had one of these at some point in time."

"It's very Brazilian." She took a drink from her own coconut and then set it down on the grass beside her, handing him one of the kabobs.

Maybe it was, but Lucas didn't feel Brazilian. Which was why he'd wanted to talk to Sophia about Marcos. If anyone knew his brother, it was her. Maybe she could help him sort through some of his conflicting emotions regarding his birth parents and his brother. He wasn't sure now was a good time, though, after what she'd just gone through at the hospital. He'd seen the hint of moisture in her eyes as she'd talked about her patient. He glanced around, letting his feet sink into the thick grass. "It's beautiful here."

"It is." She nodded. "One of my favorite places in the entire world."

He couldn't imagine having a place like this—a spot he could actually call his favorite. A strange sensation spread through his chest as he wondered if this could become one of those special places he'd want to return to again and again. He glanced at the woman next to him. Sophia's dark hair glowed with health, her cheeks finally getting some color back in them after the crisis at the hospital. Even in scrubs, she looked beautiful.

Something inside her purse buzzed just as she'd put a bite of meat in her mouth. She reached inside her bag and glanced at the readout, before handing it over to him.

Frowning, he tilted his head and she gave a couple of exaggerated chews to show she couldn't answer it then pointed at the readout.

Marcos Pinheiro, the screen read.

He pressed the talk button. "Hello?"

Silence. Then, "Who is this?" His brother's voice, true to form, bristled with suspicion.

"It's Lucas. Sophia's mouth is full at the moment, so she asked me to answer her phone."

There were several more seconds of silence before he realized his words could have been construed to something less than innocent. "We're at the park and got some food."

"Oh. Okay, good. So she's there with you."

Hadn't he just said that?

"She's right beside me. How are things there?"

"Pretty damn good. How about there? Your therapy going okay?"

He kept facing forward, not about to tell him that his therapy had just been upgraded to include a certain set of nocturnal exercises that got his heart pumping a mile a minute. Somehow he didn't think Marcos would approve, especially from his growled demand when he'd heard a man answering Sophia's phone. "Therapy's good. My stitches are out already."

"Any leads from the police?"

Why did Lucas get the feeling his brother had not called just to find out how he was doing? Especially as he'd called Sophia's cellphone. "Not yet."

"Well, I'm glad you're feeling okay." Marcos cleared his throat. "Er…what would you say if I told you I was thinking of running off to Vegas with Maggie?"

Vegas?

He was pretty sure the running-off part had nothing to do with playing the slot machines. Or maybe it did…marriage was the biggest damn gamble known to man. "That's awfully quick, isn't it?"

Sophia put her hand on his arm, her brows raised in question. He held up a finger, trying not to let his surprise at Marcos's words show on his face.

"Quick, maybe. But I've never been more certain of anything in my life."

"Wow."

What else could he say? Maggie seemed like a great woman, giving and compassionate. He'd even asked her out himself when they'd met at the medical convention a few weeks ago. He could see now how bad a match that would have been. No, he needed someone like…

He glanced at Sophia again, then looked away.

Nope, not even going there. He needed no one.

He quickly added, "Congratulations. I'm really happy for you both."

"Thanks. That means a lot to me."

Sophia tugged his arm again.

"Hold on for a second, Marcos, will you?"

He put his thumb over the receiver and held it for a second. "Marcos and Maggie are getting married."

Her mouth fell open. "Married. You're kidding!"

He wished he were. "No. Do you want to talk to him?"

"In a minute. Let me catch my breath."

Perfect. He put the phone back to his ear. "Okay, I'm back."

Marcos's voice was amused. "So what'd she say?"

"She says she's glad for you and hopes you'll have many happy years of wedded bliss."

The woman in question punched his arm hard enough to sting.

"Hmm…that doesn't sound like Sophia. She's always grumbling about my lack of fun."

Yeah, well, he didn't exactly want Marcos to know how much fun he and Sophia were currently having. In this man's bed, of all things. He made a sound he hoped sounded noncommittal.

"So, anyway, we're planning on a Vegas wedding, and we want you and Sophia to join in via a video call." He chuckled. "We figure it's as close as we can get to having you and Soph here in person. And we want you as best man and Sophia as maid of honor. The wedding chapel advertises a huge screen where we can see you as we take our vows."

A video-conferencing type of thing? Was Marcos kidding? He rolled his eyes. "I don't know, Marcos. I have no idea what Sophia's schedule is like."

The last thing he wanted to do was sit in front of a computer screen and watch his brother throw away his freedom.

Only he didn't sound shackled. The opposite, in fact.

"Sophia has that hospital wrapped around her little finger. They'll let her off. Maggie is pretty firm on wanting this, Lucas. And I'm pretty firm on doing whatever it takes to make her happy. Besides, it's been a long time since I've been able to share an important moment with my brother."

Lucas's brain glitched, sending a wave of longing rolling out through his neurons, first hitting his ears, which responded with a dull roar. He blinked hard before those signals had a chance to reach his eyes. "Okay. I'll pass the phone to her so you can talk to her."

He handed the phone over, avoiding her eyes as she took it and put it to her ear.

What else could he do other than suck it up and sit through a half-hour ceremony? Okay, this wasn't a tragedy. So he and Sophia were sleeping together. As long as they didn't say anything, no one would have to know. Things could just continue like they were now.

Even as he thought it, the rigidity of his spine began to ease and the buzzing in his head receded.

What could go wrong, right?

As soon as she got off the phone, though, he knew something was indeed wrong. "Are you okay?"

She nodded. "I'm really happy for them. Really I am."

Brushing back a lock of hair that blew over her

shoulder, he said, "I sense a 'but' in there some-where."

She bit her lip and shook her head. "It's noth-ing."

Clearly it wasn't "nothing."

He leaned forward and put his fingers beneath her chin, tilting it so she was forced to look at him. "Tell me."

"I figured Marcos would get married one day, and I can't imagine anyone better for him than Maggie, it's just…"

He waited, sensing there was something trapped inside her. Some fear about Marcos getting mar-ried. "You think it's too soon?"

"No. No, it's perfect. *Maggie* is perfect. And I've wanted this for Marcos for a long time. I just didn't think he'd do it in the States."

Why that made a difference one way or the other, he had no idea. Then it hit him like a bolt of lightning. "You're afraid he'll stay. There in the States."

She nodded and pulled her chin from his grasp. "I know it's not fair, it's just that I've known Mar-cos my entire life."

That statement sent a fiery arrow right through the center of him. "You're afraid he'll leave you."

"Not in a romantic type of way, it's never been like that between us. But if he leaves…" She drew a deep, shaky breath. "If he leaves, it means that just like those first few years at the orphanage, I'll be all…"

Her words trailed away, but Lucas could hear the rest of the sentence clanging through his skull, the noise almost deafening.

He knew what she'd been about to say with almost a hundred percent certainty. If Marcos left and moved to the United States, then, just like her days at the orphanage, she'd be all…alone.

CHAPTER FIFTEEN

"THERE ARE WORDS HERE."

Sophia traced the straight line of the medical symbol tattooed on Lucas's arm as she lay next to him in bed. Only it wasn't really a line at all. It was some kind of script.

After her almost-confession at the park, she'd leaped up, declaring that she was ready to leave. They'd gone back to the apartment, but when she'd tried to retreat to her room Lucas had taken her hand and pulled her against him, kissing her with a gentleness that had made her want to weep. He'd then led her back to the bedroom and proceeded to make love to her until she'd forgotten everything except what he made her feel.

Her body was still tingling from the encounter twenty minutes later.

"Hmm. Words where?" He tugged her leg until it was over his hip, thumb stroking her calf.

Flat on his back, and naked as the day he was born, she marveled at how he could do that. There wasn't a hint of embarrassment and because of how sure he was of himself, his confidence spilled over to her, allowing her to behave in ways she'd never dreamed possible. She felt wanton and happy tucked against his side, just as bare as he was.

"On your tattoo. Down this little line. I never noticed them before."

His thumb stopped its movement for a second before starting up again. "Yes, there are."

She squinted at the letters, trying to sound them out. *"Non Omnes Vagantes Deerant."* The words weren't English. Or Portuguese. "What does it mean?"

"It's Latin, adapted from Tolkien. It means 'Not all who wander have lost their way.'"

He dragged her on top of him with a suddenness that drove the wind from her lungs. "But the last thing I want to do right now is discuss Tolkien."

A laugh came up from her throat as she realized something was already stirring down below. The man really was insatiable. But that was all right because when she was with him, she felt pretty insatiable herself. "Okay, Dr. Carvalho, so what do you want to talk about?"

His thumb brushed the faint red mark still visible on her right breast. "I want to talk to you about this."

She went breathless. "What about it?"

Leaning up, he nipped her shoulder, then went a little lower, repeating the action, sending a shiver over her that worked its way south.

He reached her left breast, hovering over the spot that mirrored the mark on her opposite side. His tongue smoothed over her skin before his head came up. "How do you feel, Sophia, about men who bite?"

He wanted to watch.

Sophia had suggested they go together to rent formalwear for Marcos and Maggie's wedding, as it was a fairly common practice in Brazil. Seeing her in those dresses would be a mixture of torture and lust, but it was too late to back out now, even if he wanted to. Which he didn't.

Sophia had turned fiery red when the manager of the rental store had assumed they were a couple, then she'd tossed her head and given him a cheeky smile. "Do you want to see what I try on? I'll make it worth your while."

She'd already done that last night. And the night before.

Sophia was quickly becoming an addiction he just couldn't kick.

A stupid decision, but pretty much in line with every other choice he'd made lately. And hell if he didn't want to see her in that pair of killer shoes. She'd picked them up from her apartment on their way to the shop, tossing them into the back of the car, telling him those shoes had once brought Maggie a whole lot of luck.

He'd been too shocked to ask her exactly what kind of luck. Especially when her lips had curved in a secretive smile that had made his stomach tighten.

Yep, his rash decision to help her choose her outfit seemed more dangerous with every passing second.

The saleswoman measured him for a tuxedo, then led him to a red satin chair and asked him to have a seat. Feeling a little too much like a sheik or a wealthy pervert wanting his own private peep show, he sank into the chair.

It seemed to take for ever for Sophia to come out of that dressing room, but when she did…

God in heaven, when she did, it took everything in him to remain rooted in that chair. He made a point of propping an ankle nonchalantly on his knee and leaned back, although doing so set his abs on fire.

Dressed in a shiny green dress that criss-crossed over the front and revealed just a hint of cleavage, the rest of it fit her like a glove, coming to just above her knees. That left a long golden expanse of leg bare to his roving eyes until he reached the lucky shoes.

And they were every bit as mouthwatering as he'd feared. Lots of glittery straps held her foot in place and the heel was a mile high. When she turned round, the muscle in her calf stood out in sharp relief, and a sexy indentation ran along the side of her leg from just above her ankle to the bottom of her knee. Hell, he'd always been a sucker for a great pair of legs, and he knew from experience that Sophia's were strong and lithe and far too flexible for his peace of mind.

She spun back around, a smile on her face. "So? Is this the one?"

The one he wanted to peel off of her inch by inch? Oh, yeah.

"I think so."

The saleslady stepped forward. "You don't want to see any others? We have many wonderful dresses. And your wife has a beautiful figure."

Didn't she, though? Hearing the woman refer to her as his wife made something in his gut slide sideways, though, and he hurried to make that sensation go away. "She's not my wife."

Sophia shifted her weight, a slight frown marring her brow.

What the hell? "We're not married at all," he clarified further. "Not to each other and not to anyone else."

Maybe Sophia was worried that the saleslady might think they were having an affair, or that they were sneaking off to one of the country's infamous motels—which he'd heard were not for sleeping. Neither were the "drive-ins", which had no movie projectors, no white screens and no concession stands. Just a row of open bays into which you drove your vehicle, a curtain swishing closed behind you. If you'd ever had a fantasy about doing it in your car—or were simply strapped for cash—that was the place to go. Both locales were made for one thing and one thing only: fast, hard sex.

Something he shouldn't be imagining right now. Especially not with Sophia standing there in that tantalizing outfit. He could just slide the dress up those delectable thighs like he'd done with her skirt that first night and have her climb on top.

The saleslady cleared her throat, not seeming at all upset by the fact that they weren't married. "Let me put her in something else. You won't be sorry."

Sophia shook her head and took a step back, her smile nowhere to be seen. "I think this one will be fine."

Somehow he'd ruined her mood. Had it been the marriage thing? Surely she knew there couldn't be anything more than casual sex between them. Not for the long haul. He just didn't do that. *Couldn't* do that.

His gut shifted again—an angrier tightening of his innards that set his teeth on edge. He didn't want to leave the store on bad terms with her, nor did he want to leave the country that way. He wanted the good memories of their time together to follow him home. Maybe part of that was due to some misplaced jealousy over his brother's relationship with her. Maybe Lucas wanted to own an inch or two of that prime real estate that was her heart. He wasn't sure of the exact reason, but it squeezed him until he gave in.

He lowered his voice to coaxing levels. "Come

on, Soph. Just one more. Maybe something in…"
He glanced at her hair. "Red."

He knew from experience her inky-black locks
would look phenomenal flowing over the color,
since he'd seen her in a bra that very shade. It
would be hard pressed, though, to outdo the green
she had on now, as it was nothing short of heart-
stopping. There was definitely nothing wrong
with the way that dress hugged each and every
curve of the woman's body.

She wavered for a moment before her face relaxed, and she nodded. "One more." She glanced
at the saleslady. "In red, if you have something."

"Oh, yes, I have the perfect thing. Come with
me."

Sophia had felt so sure about vamping it up in
front of Lucas and having some fun with him.
Until the saleswoman had mentioned the word
"marriage." Lucas hadn't been able to set her
straight fast enough. If she'd had any doubt that
that's not how he felt about her—not how he'd
ever feel about her—she need look no further
than the consternation on his face.

So why was she here in a store dressing room,
getting ready to put on the gown of a lifetime?

She snorted. At least the thing wasn't white with a train and a veil. Who knew what kind of reaction that would have gotten? He'd have probably taken off at a sprint, injuries or no injuries.

She slid the silky red fabric over her arms, trying to decide how to get her head through the single shoulder strap that started out on the right and was supposed to go over her chest before fastening on the left in back. She finally just ducked and hoped for the best.

It worked. The dress whispered down her body like a dream, the full skirt stopping at knee level. It wasn't as revealing as the bandage-style dress she'd had on a few minutes ago, but the fabric swished over her hips, hinting at curves while not blatantly outlining them. If anything, it was sexier than the first one. She stared at her reflection. The gathered bodice clung to her breasts, the sweetheart neckline following the rounded tops perfectly then dipping in the middle. The red strap bisected her chest, providing a line that drew the eye from right to left, a set of four glittery rhinestones marking the spot where the fabric joined the dress in front and in back. Since her sandals also had a criss-cross webbing of straps punctuated with glittery dots of stones, it made the two items seem like a matched set.

It was perfect. The *dress* was perfect. But the last thing she wanted to do right now was go out and show it to Lucas.

She wasn't sure why. When the saleswoman popped her head into the room, her mouth fell open. "I knew this would suit you." She smiled. "I think your gentleman friend will be rethinking his earlier words."

Hardly. Lucas had made it perfectly clear that he wasn't interested in sticking around. She drew herself up, the thought lending her the courage necessary to smooth the dress over the fronts of her thighs and give the woman a sharp nod of her head. "No, he won't, and I don't want him to. But as he was the one who wanted to see this dress, see it he shall."

The saleswoman murmured for her to wait just a second or two and then reappeared with a pair of chandelier earrings and a wide silver cuff that she wrapped around the upper part of Sophia's left arm.

"This dress needs no necklace. Sit for just a second, please."

Sophia did as she asked, perching on the white

tufted stool, while the woman quickly pinned her hair up in a messy bun, tugging a few strands down to dance around her shoulders.

Why was she taking the time to do this? If she had some weird urge to do a little bit of match-making, then the poor woman was wasting her time. There was no match to be made here.

Even if she herself wanted it, which she didn't.

The memory of Lucas and that baby at Dr. Figuereiro's office came to mind. The kindness in his eyes as he'd smiled at the child—no hint of shock at her deformity. Just acceptance of her as she was.

He'd make a perfect father. One who would love his child no matter what.

Unlike her own family?

She swallowed. *Forget it, Sophia. He's not interested. Not now, not ever.*

A shard of hurt lodged in her chest, its pain a sharp reminder that she was still alone, no matter how many people she surrounded herself with. No matter how chaotic her job was at times. At the heart of it she'd never really had anyone to walk through life with other than Marcos, and that was all about to change now that he was getting married. While she was ecstatic for him, it just made her sense of loneliness that much harder to bear. But no one needed to know that except her.

Within another two minutes she was on her feet and headed out the door of the dressing area, her chin held high and proud.

When she stepped through the curtain, Lucas froze, his gaze trailing over her. Then his breath came through his teeth in a low whistle that told her what she already knew. The dress looked good.

He stood and moved toward her. *"Sophia, você é lindissima."*

Beautiful. He'd called her beautiful. And the verb he'd used was the one that described permanence. Not a quick "you look beautiful today" or "you look beautiful in that dress" but "you *are* beautiful"…a state of being that endured.

He took her left hand and lifted it, applying slight pressure as he urged her to turn around.

The dress wasn't particularly low in back—it hit just beneath her shoulder blades—but with her hair up, it probably made it seem like there was more skin showing than there actually was.

Something brushed against one of the earrings, sending its heavy weight swinging back and forth against her neck. The sensation made a shiver go through her. As did the warm finger sliding down her spine, from the hair at her nape to the top of the dress. Her breath caught, and she noticed the saleswoman, standing at the dressing-room door, had a knowing smile on her face.

"Beautiful," he said again, slowly turning her around to face him. When his eyes met hers, they contained that same molten glow she was coming to recognize.

He wanted her.

Catching one of her loose strands of hair, he wound it around his fingertip, tugging slightly. "Your hair looks good up."

She licked her lips. "So you like this dress better than the other one?"

"I like you. In either dress." He leaned forward until his lips were against her ear. "*Out* of either dress."

His palm cradled the line of her jaw, his thumb going beneath her chin and tilting her head back.

He was going to kiss her.

She knew it with a certainty, and suddenly she didn't care who else was in the room. She wanted his kiss. Wanted his touch. Wanted to have an out-of-dress experience.

A thread of a song came from the dressing area,

and Sophia nearly cursed aloud. Lucas pulled back, eyes narrowed on her face. She swallowed. "That's my phone. It's…um, in my purse."

"Do you want me to get it?" the saleslady asked, reminding them of her presence and bringing Sophia back to earth with a bump.

"Please." Right now, she didn't think her legs would hold her up long enough to make the trek to the dressing room.

Lucas released her and took a step back, and then another, shaking his head slightly as if trying to figure out what had happened.

Within another thirty seconds the saleslady handed her the purse. "I'll just be over there, if you need me." She motioned to a rack of dresses on the far wall.

"Thank you."

Sophia, what were you thinking?

Her phone rang again, cutting off in mid-tune this time, as whoever it was hung up. She dug around in her purse until her fingers closed around the hard plastic case. Pulling it out and glancing at the readout, she saw it was Lídia, another nurse at the hospital. She pressed redial and waited as the phone on the other end rang once…twice, then the woman answered.

"Sophia, where are you?" Her voice sounded weird. Scared, almost.

"I'm at a dress shop, why?" No reason to admit she was there with the patient she was supposed to be babysitting. One she'd been bonking every night for the past week. One for whom she'd just modeled some very sexy pieces and flashed a length of leg that should have been obscene.

"Haven't you heard the news?"

Her heart stuttered. "What news?"

"The subway—the red line near Palmeiras—derailed." There was a pause. "It's terrible, Sophia. They're saying there could be hundreds of casualties."

CHAPTER SIXTEEN

Sophia glanced at Lucas as the horror of the situation finally sank in.

His head was tilted to the side, and he stared back at her as if trying to figure out what was going on.

"Have the victims started arriving at the hospital yet?"

"No, the station is in chaos and the first responders are still in the tunnel, trying to get past the wreckage. Can you come back in? We're going to be overrun as soon as the ambulances start arriving."

"We're not far from the Palmeiras station. I have a doctor with me—maybe we can head over there and see if we can help. Once they start transporting patients, I'll come to the hospital. How many are going to be routed our way, do you know?"

"Not yet. It's rush hour. You know how tightly packed the subways are at this hour."

She did know. People jammed in until it was

impossible to fit in one more. At times it felt like the trains swallowed mouthfuls of people and then belched them out again at successive stations. "I'll check it out and call as soon as I know something."

Lídia came back, "Okay, but please be careful."

"I will."

As soon as she punched the "end call" button she quickly explained to Lucas what had happened. "I have to get over there now."

"*We* have to get over there. Like you said, I'm a doctor." He took out his wallet and peeled back some bills. "We'll be back."

The woman hesitated. "But if the dress is ruined…"

As soon as he added a few more notes, she nodded. "Don't worry about it. The dress is yours."

With no time to change back into street clothes, they hurried out of the store. When she started towards her car, Lucas stopped her, motioning toward a nearby taxi stand. "It'll be faster in one of those."

Sophia unstrapped her high heels and kicked them off her feet.

"Do you need me to run in and get your other shoes?"

"I have a pair of slip-ons in the car. I'll just grab them while you hail a cab."

By the time she'd yanked on the ballerina flats the taxi had pulled up beside her, and Lucas was out of the car, holding the door open.

She slid into the seat, and he got in beside her, motioning for the driver to be on his way.

"Does he know where we're going?"

"Yes. Evidently everyone knows what happened with the subway except us." She wasn't sure if the censure in his voice was aimed at her or at himself. But right now she didn't care. Adrenaline coursed through her system as she prepared for what was sure to be a wrenching scene. She needed to put everything out of her mind except the task at hand. People were counting on her to be at her professional best, and she owed it to them to show up with that attitude.

A warm hand reached out and gripped hers and she couldn't stop herself from leaning against Lucas, putting her head on his shoulder as she tried to draw from his strength. "All those people...trapped."

"We're going to get to them. I have credentials with Médicos Sem Fronteiras—Doctors Without Borders. They should let me in as well."

Traffic was at its crushing worst as it was every day at rush hour, but the driver was a whiz at getting in and out of the smallest places, sticking an arm out the window—hand wagging up and down—to signal whenever he wanted to move into another lane. The well-known gesture wasn't a request. It was a statement of intent: *I* am *coming over.*

Despite the driver's expertise, within two miles traffic had been reduced to a tangle of cars and snarling drivers, probably as a result of the subway accident. "It'll be faster to walk, Lucas. We're only a couple of blocks away."

She let go of his hand and started to fumble around in her purse for some money, only to have him beat her to it, handing the driver a fifty-*real* note with a murmur of thanks and a short "Keep the change."

Then they were out of the taxi and dashing between the stopped lines of traffic until they reached the sidewalk, where the distant jumble of police cars, ambulances, and fire trucks gave a grim prognostication of what they would find up ahead. The out-of-sync bursts of flashing lights only increased that feeling, like a deadly arrhythmia that was sweeping out of control.

She glanced over at Lucas. "I can run ahead if you need to slow down."

"I'm fine. Keep going."

If he was in pain, she couldn't tell. His face was a mask of determination as they continued to sprint the remaining blocks to the entrance to the subway station. Once there the crowd outside the doors pressed close, and she realized the police must be stopping people from entering. Names were being screamed out, and the sound of desperate pleading assailed her ears as relatives and friends tried to gain admittance. When the crowds grew too tight to move, Lucas grabbed her hand and edged towards the front, calmly using the size of his body to push his way through. Every stray bump of a stranger's elbow must have been agonizing for him, but he kept moving. "We're medical personnel, let us through."

Time after time, the rough statement parted the waters. When they got to the station door she saw she was right. About twenty military police were stationed in front of it, riot gear on, batons at the ready. When one of the officers glared at them when they took a step forward, Sophia yelled, "I'm from the hospital. I'm a nurse." She gestured at Lucas. "He's a doctor. We came to help."

The nearest officer motioned them forward. "I need to see some ID." If he had any thoughts about the way she was dressed, he said nothing.

Thank God she'd brought her purse. She grabbed her wallet and flipped it to the windows that held her residency card and her medical identification. Lucas flashed two different IDs as well.

It worked, because the officer scanned the documents then stepped aside. He looked her in the eye. "Rosángela Melo Medeiros, my mother, was probably on that train."

Oh, Lord. How it must hurt him to be stationed outside when all he probably wanted to do was rush inside and tear the place apart, looking for his mom. She touched his arm and repeated the woman's name. "Rosángela Melo Madeiros. I'll remember. If I see her or hear of her, I'll get word to you."

He gave a curt nod that betrayed nothing and yet said everything, then looked away, going back to the job at hand. If anyone could feel the desperation of those in the crowd, this man could. She prayed his mother was one of the lucky ones.

The escalators leading to the lower levels had been shut off, probably because of the danger below, and as she and Lucas hurried down the steps on foot, the passageway grew dimmer, the main overhead lighting switched to the emergency systems. At least there was no smoke coming up the passageway, but she did have to hold her dress bunched around her legs to keep the warm currents of air from blowing it up.

It was eerie to see the pale concrete block stairwells that led four levels underground so devoid of people. The screaming from outside hadn't followed them into the subway system itself, although she heard the distant whine of saws and other equipment. To Sophia, the lack of human voices seemed ominous, but it could just be that the train was too far inside the tunnel for much sound to make it out.

One of the first responders they met on the way down said they were working on getting the doors to the train open, and they hadn't fully assessed the number of injured, although those in the first couple of cars appeared to have borne the brunt of the impact. When she and Lucas finally reached the platform, empty stretchers were lined up in wait.

Sophia identified herself to one of the emergency workers, and he directed them to the person in charge, a burly man with a clipboard, just as the sounds of chaos from the tunnels finally reached them.

The guy pointed a pen at Lucas. "You're a doctor?"

"Yes. Reconstructive surgery, but I should be able to help."

"We're going to need all the help we can get. You up to going into that tunnel and doing triage?"

"Absolutely." Lucas glanced at Sophia. "We both are. Sophia's a trauma nurse."

The man's brow went up as he scanned her dress, obviously wondering what in the world she thought she was doing coming in like she was.

"André," he called to one of the men standing down on the tracks. Obviously the main power had been shut down or he'd have been electrocuted. "Take these two down to the train. They can help identify critical-needs patients."

As they made their way into the darkened tunnel, Lucas glanced at Sophia, glad she no longer wore the sky-high heels she'd had on at the dress shop. In the distance he could hear the sounds of machines at work…and screaming. His chest tightened, and the memory of Sophia feeding him that bite of meat came back to him, her voice telling him, "I know it may not feel like you belong here, but you have this country's blood flowing through your veins."

These were his people—and they were suffering. He quickened his step.

André spoke, having to yell to be heard over the noise. "They're trying to get the doors open. It's a mangled mess down there." Suddenly there was the sound of metal rending and then the volume of screaming increased with a suddenness that made Lucas pause. When a strange kind of rhythmic thud hit his ears, along with distant grunts, he realized what it was. The doors were open and people were leaping off the trains willy-nilly and onto the tracks. The thought sent a chill through him.

Sophia said the trains were packed to overflowing at rush hour. So if passengers started pouring off the trains, they'd have to come by the three of them to reach the station that lay behind them.

The shouts grew louder, mashing together into a single unit of sound. Closing in at a rapid pace. Lucas glanced back the way they'd come. They'd never make it to the platform before the first wave of passengers reached them. He could pray that everyone was filing out in an orderly fashion, but if he knew human nature they would be rushing towards safety. Heaven help anyone in their path.

He gripped Sophia's hand and hauled her towards him and shouted at the worker who was leading them into the bowels of the tunnel. "We need to get against one of the walls, so we don't get trampled."

Even as he said it, in the distance he saw shadows—bouncing forms that had no real shape, but there were a lot of them. Heading towards them at frightening speed. "Now!"

As if realizing what he meant, André's eyes widened then his head swiveled towards the back of the tunnel, just like Lucas's had done seconds earlier. Putting an arm around Sophia's waist, Lucas pulled her to the nearest concrete wall and pressed her into it, wrapping his body half around her so the crowds would reach him first. Then he braced his feet wide, made sure André had heeded his warning as well, and waited for the tsunami to hit.

Panicked eyes were the first thing he saw, all filled with the same desperate fear. Then something struck his shoulder and swept by him. Again and again, the deafening sounds of terror accompanied the slap of human flesh, the blows almost dislodging him several times and sending pain ricocheting through his injuries.

They'd promised to try to locate the police officer's mother. That hope was all but dead now. He tucked Sophia's head into his shoulder, desperate to keep her safe, as more and more people swept by, the frenetic pace slowing as the numbers grew, the mass—like an oil slick—spreading further and further out to the sides. Lucas squeezed as tight as he dared without crushing Sophia against the wall, and prayed it would be enough to keep them both from being trampled or worse. Because if one of them lost their balance and fell—or if one of the passengers caught Lucas's shoulder hard enough and spun him sideways and into the stream of bodies, it would be all over. One or both of them could die.

CHAPTER SEVENTEEN

THEY WERE STILL ALIVE.

He lifted his head, trying to figure out how long they'd been standing there. Fifteen minutes? Longer? People were still moving past them, but the numbers were beginning to thin—the pace slowing, as those at the back of the line were evidently less frantic than those at the front.

His body felt like it had a couple of weeks ago right after his surgery. And he was pretty sure he'd be covered with bruises from head to toe. But he was still breathing. He glanced down at where Sophia stood with her arms curled over the back of her head. Touching one of her hands, he was relieved when she straightened from her position.

"Are you okay?" His voice was hoarse and he had to clear his throat and ask again in a louder voice.

Sophia nodded and turned her head sideways to look up at him. "A little scratched from the wall, but I think I'll live." Her eyes narrowed a bit as she studied him. "Did you get hit in the head?"

"I don't think so, why?"

"Your left eye is turning purple. I can't tell if it's injured or just dirt from the tunnel."

He scrubbed it against his shoulder, wincing as a dull ache went through the socket. Nope, he was going to have a shiner. Hell, he didn't remember getting hit that hard. "It'll be fine."

He glanced to the other side, where André had been, and found the spot empty.

A wave of nausea hit the pit of his stomach. His eyes swept the tracks where people still trickled by and spotted the worker standing with his arms outstretched as if guarding something.

Or someone.

"Stay here for a minute," he muttered to Sophia.

His relief at seeing the man ended when he noticed two people on the floor.

One of the figures was crouched beside someone else.

A child?

The crowds were sparse enough now that they were splitting down the middle and streaming on either side of André, keeping the tiny group safe for the moment. Lucas maneuvered his way towards them little by little, trying to be careful not to injure anyone else in the process.

Once there, he gave the man's shoulder a squeeze. "Good job."

The worker glanced at him, his cheek smeared with dirt. "I saw the two go down…wasn't sure I'd be able to make it to them in time."

"You probably saved their lives. If you can stand guard a few minutes longer, I'll take a look."

Not waiting for the other man to respond, he knelt beside the pair. The person on the floor was indeed a child…a girl around six years old, her eyes open and glassy-looking, a huge knot on the right side of her forehead. There was a shoe-shaped smudge on the white blouse of what looked like a school uniform.

A man's footprint.

Lucas's head filled with a buzzing sound, his vision turning red for a second or two. What was wrong with people?

Even as he thought it, he knew his anger wasn't entirely fair. He'd treated trample injuries from concert venues or in natural disasters before. Sometimes people were so tightly packed against one other that they were swept along without any real control over their movements. Those in front were propelled forward by those behind them, until the whole group moved as a single entity. If someone fell, there was often no way to stop and help them. He'd worked on facial lacerations from just such situations. Worse, it was a horrible way to die.

Thankfully, this girl wasn't dead. Or maimed. But she was injured.

Sophia knelt beside them as well, making him frown. "I thought I told you to stay where you were."

"I can think for myself." Her eyes were on the still figure of the little girl, and she reached down to brush her fingers across her hair. "Is she okay?"

"I was just checking her." He didn't have his medical kit or a way to test her pupillary reactions, but he was going to bet she had a head injury. Whether it was a simple concussion or a fracture could only be determined at a hospital. Leaning down, he peered at her eyes, carefully noting that neither pupil was blown, both appearing to be the same size.

When she groaned and started to move, Lucas murmured to her in what he hoped was a reassuring tone, asking her to lie still. He glanced at the woman, whose brown eyes were streaming with tears. "Are you her mother?"

The woman nodded. "I—I was holding her, but someone pushed me and she slid down. I couldn't find her."

Sophia touched her shoulder. "It's not your fault. We're here to help you both." She picked up the girl's hand and pressed it into her mother's. "Try to keep her calm while we make sure she's okay."

The mother, who'd seemed as stunned as the girl a minute or two ago, took a deep breath and nodded.

As if she knew exactly what he wanted her to do, Sophia took the girl's other hand, allowing Lucas to assess her without worrying about whether or not the child was going to twist away from his touch. Starting at her shoulders, he ran his hands down her arms, feeling for obvious fractures. So far so good. He wanted a backboard, though, to stabilize her neck and spine.

Her ribs felt intact as well, and he watched for any reaction to the steady pressure of his hands, but other than that moan she'd given a few seconds ago she was calm. Maybe a little too calm.

Her belly felt soft, another good sign. Despite

the shoeprint on her shirt, maybe there'd been no real damage done.

Then he found it.

The second his fingers skated over her thigh through the fabric of her skirt, he felt a hard, uneven ridge that he immediately identified.

Bone.

It had missed coming through the girl's skin by just a hair. He caught Sophia's eye, and her brows lifted in question as if knowing he'd found something. "Hold her steady."

She didn't ask what was wrong, just nodded. Lucas tried not to think about how she seemed to anticipate his every move, about how well they worked together. He forced himself to concentrate on the job at hand instead.

The last thing he wanted to do was frighten the mother. Or the child, who could thrash around and push the bone through. If that happened, bacteria from the tunnel could enter the open wound, or the sharp edges of the bone could shred an artery. If either of those things happened, they were in big trouble.

"André," he called to the man still standing guard above them. "I need something to use as a splint. I'll hold your position, if you can find me something straight."

Lucas knew there were probably worse injuries on the trains themselves, and he wanted to get to those passengers as soon as possible, but he also needed to secure the girl's leg before he handed her off to the next batch of people.

Before the other man could answer, the first sign of help appeared in the tunnel. Several EMTs jogged toward the train, carrying stretchers. Must have been the ones they'd seen waiting on the platform. One of the medical workers stopped beside them. "What have you got?"

The man didn't question Lucas's right to be there, just jumped in to help as if he were someone he worked with every day.

"Fractured right femur and possible head trauma."

"Right." The EMT squatted beside them. "Anything worse in the trains themselves?"

Lord, he hoped not. "I haven't been able to get down there yet."

"I'll stabilize her if you want to head over there, Doc," the guy said.

"Great." Lucas glanced at Sophia, not wanting to leave her.

"Go," she said. "I'll find you later."

He nodded then leaned over to kiss her, his hand grazing her cheek before standing to his feet. His glance touched the little girl on the ground. At least she had a mom to stand guard over her. One who'd refused to leave, even though she herself could have been trampled in the process.

He wondered what Sophia was thinking at this very second. Was she remembering her own parents, who'd abandoned her over an injury that was easily repaired? Who might have even left her in a tunnel very much like this one to fend for herself?

He didn't want to leave—wanted to be that guy who would stick around, who would be there for her no matter what.

He couldn't. Not now. Not in a few weeks when he'd have to head back home.

She can take care of herself. She's done it her whole life.

If that was supposed to make him feel better, it didn't. He climbed to his feet, addressing the medical worker. "Okay. I'll go see what I can do."

"Appreciate it," the EMT said.

He hurried down the tunnel, following another stretcher, the procession of empty ones filling him with foreboding about what he'd find when he got to the train. Then he forced every thought out of his head except for the job at hand. And prayed things were not going to be as bad as he feared. But when he arrived at the first twisted subway car, the smear of a bloody handprint on the window, accompanied by low moans from multiple directions, told him he was wrong.

It was going to be every bit as terrible as he'd feared. And worse.

Lucas glanced at his watch as he handed off his last patient to a waiting volunteer. Eight hours had passed and they were finally able to attend to the least injured of the victims.

One of the medical workers nodded to him as he passed by and Lucas lifted a hand in a quick wave. He'd been surprised at how easily he'd been accepted by everyone. Despite his accent, they'd worked beside him, accepting his recommendations for treatment without question. It made him feel…needed. Wanted.

He jumped from the car onto the tracks and leaned back to stretch his back, every muscle in his body stiff and sore.

He didn't know the exact number of fatalities but there were a lot. The dead had been laid out in rows side by side in one of three cars and covered with anything the workers could get their hands on. Including Lucas's shirt, which had been used to drape the face of a boy who was similar in age to the girl he'd treated in the tunnel. Only this boy's head injuries had been catastrophic. The only blessing was that death had probably been instantaneous. A hollow ache settled in his chest as he wondered if the child's parents had been killed as well. The scene had been so jumbled, appearing as if people had been thrown around the cars like rag dolls. No one was certain who belonged to whom. The terrible task of identifying the dead and injured would fall to frantic relatives.

Some would rejoice. Others would mourn.

Several of the patients he'd attended were extremely critical. Who knew if they'd even made it to the hospital.

He'd only seen Sophia twice during that time, but just in passing—there'd evidently been no opportunity for her to leave and go to the hospital, as she'd promised Lídia, she'd been needed here at the accident site. But in the last two hours he hadn't seen her at all. They were down to people with minor wounds, and now that he had time to take a breath, he found he missed her.

That's just the exhaustion talking.

He knew it was the case, but it didn't help fill the hole in his gut.

Hell. Maybe it was time for him to go home.

Not to Marcos's apartment, but home to the States, before whatever was going on with him got any further out of hand. Before he made a promise that he *couldn't* keep.

Moving gingerly down the tracks, he noted most of the people milling around now were official-looking folk with clipboards. Inspectors, probably, trying to assess the cause of the accident.

Further down, he spotted someone resting against the dirty concrete wall of the tunnel, a dark jacket wrapped around her, a strip of red cloth peeking out below it.

Sophia.

His chest cramped and he wasn't sure whether it was with relief or some other emotion. Someone had evidently loaned her a coat. For some reason, he wanted it to be *his* jacket she wore, even though he had nothing to give her at the moment. Not even a shirt. Was that how Marcos had felt when he'd handed over his own flip-flops and insisted he put them on? Had his brother felt this fierce protectiveness that seared his insides and coated his throat?

No, it wasn't the same at all.

He had no claim over Sophia. But it did make him realize something. Despite her parents' abandonment, there were people who would reach out to her. Sophia was strong, she'd proven that time and time again, but there was also a delicate vulnerability to her that tugged at him. Made him want to keep her far from anything that might hurt her. Judging from the coat she wore, he wasn't the only one touched by that side of her.

She saw him, and her eyes lit up, making another part of him ache.

Pushing away from the wall, she came towards him.

He put his arm around her waist, not sure if he was supporting her or if it was the other way around. "I thought you'd have left by now."

She shook her head. "I wanted to make sure there wasn't anything else I could do to help."

"I think we've done all we can." His fingers tightened, pulling her a bit closer, the feel of her softness molding to him like a balm in the midst of tragedy. "Let's go home."

Suddenly he knew that he wanted nothing more

than to hold her. Kiss her. Erase the horror of what he'd seen, if only for a few short hours. He'd make no promises. And if she didn't want him after today, he'd back away for ever.

He was probably being selfish. But as he leaned down and dropped a kiss onto her temple, her warm scent obliterating the smell of fear and death, it was the only thing he wanted to do.

She tilted her head and allowed him to graze her lips with his. He had to fight not to deepen the contact. Not to press her against the wall of the tunnel and prove to himself that they were both here. Both alive and unharmed.

As if she could sense exactly what he was thinking, she murmured against his mouth, "Take me home, Lucas. Please."

CHAPTER EIGHTEEN

SOPHIA SHUDDERED AS Lucas slowly unzipped her dress, his every move reflected in the bathroom mirror in front of them.

The expensive garment was covered in dirt and blood, as was her hair. Her skin. It was as if the misery and terror of a thousand people were ground into her soul and could never be washed away.

She reached down so she could pull the dress over her head, only to have him stop her with a murmur. "You did this for me when I couldn't do it for myself. It's time I did it for you."

He'd taken her clothes off many times over the last several days, but this felt different. Somber. Weightier. Maybe because of the tragedy.

The tenderness as his hands slid down her arms made her breath catch, and when he linked his fingers with hers, giving a gentle squeeze, her stomach twisted.

His gaze came up, meeting hers in the reflective surface. One of his eyes was indeed black and blue, and would probably be even worse tomorrow. It looked like he'd been in the fight of his life, rather than fighting for the lives of others.

He was strong and kind.

And she loved him.

She swallowed. *Deus*. She loved him.

She was supposed to have kept this light and fun. A quick fling while he was recovering from surgery.

It was supposed to be all about the sex.

When had that changed? During their time in the subway tunnel, when he'd cared for that little girl? Or had she been headed this way from the moment he'd strode towards her in a hospital gown?

It didn't matter. What did matter was that he was here with her now. Surely he couldn't touch her like he was and not feel *something*. It was on the tip of her tongue to ask, but she didn't, fearing if she was wrong he'd recoil in horror. She couldn't bear it if he turned away from her right now, when she needed him so very much.

Letting go of her hands, he tugged the dress up and over her head, leaving her in just her bra and panties.

He leaned down and kissed the side of her neck, his body moving in behind hers. She shivered as his heat enveloped her, warming a tiny portion of her heart, filling her with hope as she remembered the tender way he'd held her hand and led her from the tunnel—the soft press of his lips as he'd kissed her temple. How a few days ago he'd told her to say goodbye while sounding very much like he'd wanted her to stay.

He had to care at least a little, right?

"Stay here while I turn on the shower." He whispered the words against her ear, his teeth teasing her lobe.

It was obvious where this was headed. If she was going to salvage some portion of her heart, she needed to stop it now.

Only she didn't want to. She wanted to see if she could tell anything from the way he took her. Instead of walking into the shower enclosure, though, he opened the door to the bathroom and left.

Sophia frowned in confusion, until he returned with a square packet. Okay, so he was thinking more clearly than she was. She turned around, leaning a hip against the counter to watch him undo his belt, his shirt already long gone, left behind in the subway tunnel. The remnants of his gunshot wounds stood out against his tanned skin, making her chest ache. He'd been through so much since coming to Brazil.

"How are you feeling?" she asked.

"Sore. Tired."

"Then…?" she motioned toward the condom he'd tossed on the counter, wondering if she was wrong.

His lips curved. "Not that sore. Not that tired." His smile faded as his eyes ran over her. "The only thing I want right now is you, Sophia."

Her stomach clenched at the way he said it. Surely the intensity she heard in his voice meant something. He wanted her. *Her.* Some part of him had to care.

"I want you too, Lucas. I do."

He moved toward her and laid his hands on the countertop on either side of her hips. His cheeks slid along hers. "You have no idea what those words do to me."

Oh, yes, she did, if they were anything like what his had done to her.

She slid her arms under his and folded them over his back, holding him close and pressing a kiss to his shoulder, next to the scar from his surgery. The way his breath hissed in at her touch made her smile.

She did that to him. She tried it again, adding just the barest hint of her teeth this time.

Lucas stepped back with a grunt. "I need to get that shower running, or you're going to have to take me sweaty and filthy."

She'd take him any way she could get him, but she let him go. He undid his pants and rolled them down his hips, along with his briefs.

Whew. He was already hard. Ready.

She was ready, too. She reached back and started to undo her bra, only to stop when he slowly shook his head.

"Don't. I want that."

Deus. Lowering her hands and wrapping them around her waist, she waited as he switched on the water. When he came back, he had droplets clinging to his dark eyelashes, running down his strong chest. All she wanted to do was lap the moisture up with her tongue.

He didn't give her a chance. Crowding her back against the counter, his hand skimmed up her back until he reached the hair at her nape. Gathering it in his hand, he tugged her head back and held it there for a second or two as if to show her that she was completely at his mercy.

She was.

He enthralled her. Seduced her. Held her very heart in the palm of his hand.

He could do anything he wanted to her right now, and she'd let him.

His lips touched her chin. Swept along the line of her jaw. Edged down the side of her neck until he reached the joint where it met her shoulder. Lips became teeth as he pressed into her skin with enough force to wring a moan from her, a series of shudders racking her body.

He held on as his fingers reached up and flicked open the clasp to her bra. When he let the strapless garment drop to the floor, he finally came up and claimed her mouth in a searing kiss that left her reeling and clutching his arms for support.

Somewhere in the back of her head she was aware that her feet were slowly moving forward as Lucas continued to kiss her, as his tongue swept into her mouth and taunted her with long, slow strokes.

Then a warm stream of water cascaded over her head, making her gasp. Lucas pulled away with a smile, taking hold of her shoulders and turning her away from him. He leaned his chin on her shoulder for a second or two before reaching for a bottle of body wash on the rack in front of them. The feeling of being enveloped by him was made stronger when—his arms still around her—he tipped the container and squirted a generous amount onto one of his palms. Returning the soap to its spot, he slowly rubbed his hands together and placed them on either side of her belly, the lather making a sudsy trail across her skin as he inched his way up toward her breasts, hands circling ever higher.

"Your skin is soft. Like silk."

The firm, insistent press of a certain part of his anatomy against her lower back said she wasn't the only one affected by his touch. And even though she knew where he was headed, her breath still caught in her throat when his hands curved over her breasts, fingers brushing her nipples. Instead of lingering there, like she was aching for him to do, he moved higher, still smoothing the layer of suds across her body. Along her collarbone, up the line of her throat.

"I need more soap," he murmured, his chin never leaving its perch. The rush of warm air against her neck was heady. "Can you reach the bottle?"

She leaned forward, noting that he followed her movements with ease. Expecting him to hold out his hand, she was puzzled when his palms slid up and down her arms instead.

"Open the cap."

She did as he asked, fumbling a bit but finally managing to get the thing open. Still he remained where he was.

Did he want her to return the favor? She started to pour it into her hand, only to have him stop her. "Not there."

He wrapped his hand around hers and directed her to the spot just over her left breast. "Right here."

He wanted her to pour it over herself? Gulping when he let go of her hand, she tipped the bottle and let the liquid drizzle in a stream down her breast, practically melting when it ran over the tip of her nipple and continued down toward her stomach.

"Nice." His hand came up and worked the soap into the sensitive peak. "Now the other side."

She wasn't sure she could—felt drunk with the pleasure of what he was doing. And just as she started to turn the bottle he squeezed the nipple he was working on, causing the soap to dribble onto the floor, instead of hitting her body.

"Oh, Sophia. You missed." He bit the side of her neck, and she almost dropped the bottle altogether. "You'll have to do better than that. Try again." The last two words were growled against her ear.

Her breath huffed in and out of her lungs, and she felt less confident with every second. But his fingers had eased up and were now stroking in soothing motions over her soapy breast. So she tried to do it in a hurry this time, only to have him do the same thing, fingers gripping the most sensitive part of her breast and sending a shock of electricity arching straight to her center.

"Ah!" The sound came out as a cry as her hand squeezed hard against the soap bottle and sent a jet of it shooting out into space.

He swore against her ear, his erection jerking against her back. "Hell." Reaching around, he took the container from her. "You, young lady, are sending all kinds of thoughts spinning through my head."

The soap turned in her direction and with quick, rhythmic squeezes Lucas sent spurts of the creamy white liquid against her breasts, her stomach, her inner thighs. The act was obscene and erotic all at once, and she immediately grasped what kind of thoughts he was talking about.

Yes! She wanted that. Wanted him on her. Marking her as his.

Twisting in his arms, her fingers swept down his sides until she found what she wanted. Hot and hard in her hands, she reveled in the feeling of power as a tremor went through him. She gave him a slow smile. "I need some of that soap, only *my* hands are full this time." She slid them in a long, slow stroke over his engorged flesh. "Right here."

His eyes blazed as he lowered the bottle and allowed it to flow over her hands, over his own skin. She stroked and squeezed, trying to drive him as crazy as he'd driven her seconds ago. Still holding him, she allowed the rush of water to wash away the suds.

A groan sounded above her, and when she glanced up, his eyes were closed, his head leaning back against the tiles.

Now was her chance.

Being as quiet as she could, she kept stroking him as she got to her knees in front of him. Her mouth watered. She'd barely gotten a chance to look at him during their time together, and had certainly not gotten to taste him.

Leaning forward, she opened her mouth and engulfed the head of his penis, hearing a sharp grunt above her, followed by the sound of her name.

His hands went to the back of her head, fingers tunneling into her hair. But instead of pulling her away like he had on other occasions, he pressed her closer. A thrill went through her as she willingly went down to the limit of her endurance and came back to gulp a quick breath of air before moving forward again.

She'd never done this to a man, and was surprised at how fierce her own pleasure was as she allowed her tongue to stroke down his length and swirl around him, trying to keep a steady rhythm going.

She heard him muttering above her, a combination of what she thought were English swear words and supplications as she continued to try to take him deeper and deeper. A few seconds later, his grip on her hair tightened, and he hauled her away from him, the popping sound as he left her mouth ringing through the space around them. He went down on his haunches in front of her and cupped her cheeks, then kissed her, long and deep, his tongue pressing into her mouth again and again as if he had to finish what she'd started.

She'd wanted to finish him. Was disappointed that he hadn't let her.

The feeling didn't last long, though, because as soon as his mouth left hers he dragged her to her feet and ripped open with his teeth the condom he'd brought into the shower. As soon as it was on, he turned her to face the shower wall. "Spread your legs for me."

Deus.

She shuffled her feet apart, her right cheek pressed tight against the tiles. And almost as soon as she did so he bent his knees and found her, pushing home in a rush.

"Hell. I've been thinking about this." He pulled out and thrust deep again, driving the air from her lungs. "Every second of every day. You drive me crazy."

How could he even form words? Her mind was a mush of rolling waves that carried her up high and then dropped her, before starting to climb once again.

Time and time again he pressed her into the wall, his lips at her ear, breath rough as he bathed her in incoherent sounds that she instinctively knew were meant for her alone.

She'd wanted him to mark her. Well, he was. With each pump of his flesh into her he was branding her as his, her body instinctively gripping each time he entered her as if to bind him to her.

One of his hands found her breast, while the other slid between the tile wall and her stomach before moving to the V between her legs, his thumb finding her most sensitive spot and stroking over it.

"Lucas."

"I'm right here." As if to prove it he moved deep. So deep. Pressing against some inner part of her as his thumb continued to move in tight circles. He didn't let up, and although it felt like his body was tense and still behind her, the pressure inside her static, there was a rhythmic push and release happening that drove her wild.

It was too much. Not enough.

His fingers kept moving below and above, then suddenly he clamped down on her nipple as well as the nub between her legs.

The shaft of pleasure was shattering in its intensity, spearing straight down with a single thrust that wrenched a scream from her. Her body went off all at once, fierce spasms taking her inner muscles by storm.

Lucas's shout hit her ears at almost the same time, his body moving frantically to keep up with hers, driving into her again and again.

When her brain finally re-engaged, she realized they were both on the shower floor, both on all fours. Lucas's body was around hers. In hers. Touching her inside and out.

She wanted this man. More than she'd wanted anything in her life.

Please, want me, too, Lucas. Please.

Something inside her broke on a sob that came out before she could stop it. He stiffened above her as another and then another came out, leaving her helpless to staunch the flow. She had no idea why she was crying, whether it was with happiness or grief, but Sophia knew one thing was true.

What had passed between them was irrevocable. There was no going back. And as that thought wormed its way into her mind, so did a sense of despair. She had given absolutely everything she had to give, and then he'd wrung even more from her. More than she'd ever dreamed possible.

Whatever happened between them after this

didn't matter. Whether it was good or bad, it would change nothing.

Because she would never be the same ever again.

CHAPTER NINETEEN

HE'D MADE HER CRY.

Sophia lay curled into him, one long, slim leg over his thigh, her slow, even breathing telling him she was asleep.

He'd tried to get her to talk to him, but she'd insisted it was nothing, just the aftermath of the subway accident, followed by what had happened between them in the shower.

It was normal, she'd insisted, as if she cried every time she made love.

That was a lie. She hadn't cried the other times they'd been together. And he sure as hell didn't want to think of her getting this emotional with someone else.

After turning off the shower, he'd somehow carried her to the bed, despite his injuries, and held her as she continued to cry until she'd finally been limp against him. Her sobs had given way to hiccups, which had remained long after her tears had stopped flowing.

His heart raged inside him. At first he'd thought he'd hurt her somehow by going too deep with his thrusts. That had changed as he'd realized the heartbroken sounds hadn't been from pain but had been due to something else entirely. He may not have hurt her physically but he sure as hell had done something to her emotionally.

He hadn't made her any promises, so it wasn't that. And she'd refused to discuss it. Had finally just fallen asleep with moisture still on her cheeks. He'd pressed her face to his shoulder, his hand stroking along the silky skin of her back as he'd tried to think about what his next move should be. He wanted to fix it—whatever "it" was—but had a feeling nothing he did would help.

Dammit! He'd never been at a loss for words before. Never felt so unsure about what he should do.

Lucas gently slipped from beneath her leg and got up, holding his breath as he prayed she wouldn't stir. Her hand reached out for a second… found his pillow and clutched it tight.

His throat spasmed as he watched her for a minute or two.

The urge to get back under the covers and gather her to him swept over him, the urge so strong he clenched his hands into tight fists to refrain from acting on it.

Breathing hard, he had no idea what was happening to him, but he had to get away from this bed right now.

Going into the bathroom, Lucas braced his hands on the marble countertop in the bathroom, staring at the fresh red scars on his shoulder and abdomen. When he moved his arm to look closer, his tattoo caught his eye. He ran his index finger down the black staff that lay at the heart of the rod of Asclepius symbol, remembering how Sophia had stroked across it just like that.

Everyone noticed his father's name and the words "Promises Kept" that he'd had inked onto his flesh. But like the faint scar on Sophia's lip, very few people ever saw the extra words he'd had inscribed down the length of the staff a few years ago, or they wrongly assumed the black Latin words were part of the ornate design.

Not Sophia. She'd seen them—had asked what they meant.

Not all who wander have lost their way.

The wording was slightly different from Tolkien's original quote, but Lucas had thought it fit him to a T—an explanation of his nomadic lifestyle.

Only right now Lucas wondered if he'd been lying to himself all along. Because a part of him felt untethered, aimless…lost.

Being in Sophia's arms last night had felt strangely like coming home. He hadn't wanted to leave them. Ever.

Only he couldn't afford to stay.

He had commitments back in the States. And he couldn't pretend to be someone he wasn't. If he stuck around, he'd eventually hurt her. Again.

Dr. Figuereiro's offer popped into his mind. He immediately dismissed it. He never stayed in one place for more than a few years at a time—and that type of job required a commitment that was beyond him. Not that he'd ever tried it but, still, it wouldn't work. He'd eventually want to leave for parts unknown. And then he'd hurt a lot more people than just Sophia—those hundreds of photographs on the good doctor's wall were evidence of that.

You need to leave. Now. While you still can.

Before you do something that will hurt her even more further down the line.

Dressing quickly, he picked up his wallet and

stuffed it into his back pocket. When he moved to the doorway, he caught sight of Sophia's dress lying crumpled on the floor. Once a vibrant red, the fabric was stained with dirt and blood from the rescue efforts at the subway. It was battered and bruised. Barely recognizable.

He glanced back at Sophia and wondered if what they'd done last night had left her feeling like that discarded dress. God, he hoped not.

The memory of peeling that garment off her body came back to him.

You did this for me when I couldn't do it for myself. It's time I did it for you.

Hadn't his brother done the same thing when they'd been kids? Helped him do things he hadn't been able to do for himself?

Was that why he had chosen to work with underprivileged children? Trying to pay Marcos back over and over for the sacrifices he'd made on his behalf?

Maybe it was time he actually did something for his brother.

Like stand beside him as he took his marital vows?

He scooped up the dress and held it to his face for several long seconds. He might not be able to make things right with Sophia but he could at least try to fix one thing. With a heart full of lead he made his way to the front door, leaving his set of keys on the side table. He then let himself out of the house…and out of Sophia's life.

"He said to do whatever it took to make it right."

The dry cleaner handed Sophia the garment bag containing her dress. A dangerous prickling started behind her eyes, but she straightened her spine.

She would not allow herself to cry. Not right now.

Waking up to find Lucas gone had been just about the worst thing she could imagine. He'd left no note. No nothing. The second she'd seen his set of keys, though, she'd known. He had gone, and he wasn't coming back.

She'd been shocked when the cleaner had called the next day to say her dress was ready. Dress? She'd told the woman she must be mistaken, she hadn't taken anything in to be dry-cleaned. When the clerk had mentioned the color and said a gentleman with an American accent had brought it in, her heart had contracted. Maybe he'd left a note with the dress.

"D-did he say anything? The man who brought in the dress?"

"Just what I said. That he wanted me to do whatever it took to make it right. Money was no object."

Money was no object.

If anything should set her back on her feet, it was that. Lucas wanted to be back in the States, back at his practice where he had the kind of life most people only dreamed of.

She'd been a fool to even hope he might want to stay here in Brazil. Stay with her. He didn't love her. Had never even hinted that he felt anything for her but lust. He'd fulfilled his end of the bargain, giving her a few wildly sensual nights that she would never forget. It wasn't his fault that she'd fallen in love with him.

But if he didn't care at all, why had he bothered sending her dress to be fixed? Guilt?

No, he had nothing to feel guilty for, as she'd never confessed her feelings.

The dress wasn't the only thing that confused her. Lucas's lovemaking had seemed different that last night. Enough for her to hope that he might feel something for her, too.

She murmured her thanks to the dry cleaner and

then made her way out of the shop, still trying to sort through her jumbled emotions.

Marcos's wedding was in a week, and he'd called that morning to make sure she'd still be able to video-call. No one had mentioned Lucas, and she wondered if his brother even knew that he was back in the States.

The one good thing that had come out of the accident was that she'd been at the hospital almost nonstop over the last couple of days. But now that more victims were being released, her hours would soon slack off again, which meant she'd have way too much time to think.

She needed to take a break. Do something to force her out of the funk she was sinking into. Lucas had only been in her life a short time. She refused to spend the rest of it reliving each and every word he'd said and trying to read something into it. It would have been better if he'd just faced her and told her flat out that he was done—that he was headed home. Instead, he'd slunk away without a word. That didn't sound like the supremely confident man she'd come to know over the last couple of weeks.

So why didn't she figure out a way to ask him

once and for all why he'd left like he had? Maybe then she could move past this chapter.

The idea grew until she couldn't see beyond it.

The man owed her an explanation. And she intended to get it.

With her chin held high and the bag over her arm, she made a decision. If her dress could be fixed, so could she. She knew just what to do to start that process.

First, she was changing jobs. It was high time she started thinking about someone other than herself and the way she saw it, Dr. Figuereiro's office was the perfect place to do that. And, second, she was going to call in a favor from a friend. If anyone could figure out a way to make this happen, it was Marcos.

Why had he thought this was a good idea?

Standing beside Marcos and Maggie in the wedding chapel, Lucas fiddled with his bow tie. He didn't really have a choice. He'd taken Sophia's advice and talked to Marcos about their past. They'd settled quite a few issues—well, as much as anyone could hope for with a brother who hadn't been able to think about anything other than his bride-to-be.

Besides, if he'd told Marcos why he didn't want to stand beside him as his best man, he'd probably have more than just a black eye. And from what he'd heard, Sophia hadn't even hesitated about taking part in the ceremony, so maybe he'd made a mountain out of a molehill. Maybe she hadn't been affected at all.

Unlike him, who hadn't gotten much sleep since he'd left Brazil a week ago. Every time he nodded off, images of Sophia came and tormented him with hints of what might have been.

But it couldn't be. Not for him. There was no way he could hold someone's happiness in his hands and be expected to keep it safe. He wasn't made that way.

Was he?

Marcos jabbed him with an elbow. "You okay?"

"Yeah. Sure." He yanked on his tie again, wondering if he'd ever get rid of this strangling sensation.

Probably not. Maybe he could just work longer hours, make more volunteer trips.

And risk hurting a patient because he was too tired to function?

No. That wasn't the answer.

Then what was?

If he knew, he'd be in a whole lot better shape than he was.

He forced his mind back to the task at hand and glanced at the happy couple. Maggie was beautiful in a cream lace dress that hugged her slender curves. His brother was obviously head over heels in love with her, if the protective arm around her waist and appreciative stares were anything to go by.

All Lucas wanted to do was get this wedding over with and get out of there. He hadn't really expected to lay eyes on Sophia ever again—and the thought of seeing her image on that enormous screen in front of them was twisting his gut into hard little knots.

And yet the thought of *not* seeing her made his throat clog with emotions he didn't understand.

The minister walked in and greeted them. "I understand we're going to place a video call to Brazil?"

"Yes, we'd like a close friend to take part in our wedding."

More than a close friend. At least, for Lucas. He felt more for her than he'd ever felt for anyone in his life.

Was this love?

He clenched his jaw. No. It couldn't be.

Then why was he suddenly so anxious to see her that he could hardly breathe as they punched the numbers into the machine?

He stared at the screen as the phone on the other end buzzed twice. Three times. Four. Five. Out of the corner of his eye he saw Maggie glance at Marcos, who squeezed her hand.

"She'll be here," he said.

He sent Lucas a pointed look. Although he hadn't shared everything with his brother, he had confessed that a few things had happened that shouldn't have. His brother had put two and two together and come up with five: that Lucas had broken his childhood friend's heart, and if that was the case, Marcos was going to break him.

But he hadn't broken her heart. Right?

So why the hell had she been crying?

It couldn't have been heartbreak, because he'd been right there with her. Had spent most of the night with her. No, her tears had seemed to come from what had transpired between them in the shower. It's what had helped propel him out the door.

The minister clicked cancel after the tenth ring.

"Do you want to go on without her, or should I try again?"

"Try again." There was an ominous rumble to his brother's voice as he glanced toward the back of the chapel at the doorway. Surely he wasn't thinking of skipping out.

Evidently the minister sensed something was wrong as well, looking a little nervous as he hit redial.

That was nothing compared to the rock in the pit of Lucas's stomach.

The phone rang again. Once. Twice.

The sound of running feet came from behind them, the clickety-clack of high heels unmistakable.

"Sorry I'm late."

Every ounce of air left Lucas's lungs as he swung round to find Sophia hurrying up the aisle of the small chapel.

She stopped for a second, and they stared at each other.

The woman was gorgeous. Cheeks flushed. Hair pulled up into soft curls on her head.

That red dress.

His throat tightened further. She'd gotten it from

the cleaners. Had worn it, even after he'd left her without a word of explanation.

And she was here. In the States.

Sophia jerked her eyes from his and went over to Maggie, hugging her tight. "Sorry. The card key at the hotel was different than I'm used to. I couldn't figure out how to make it work."

Lucas hadn't been able to figure out how to make it work either. And he wished to hell he could.

He wanted her attention back. But she smiled at Maggie and then hugged Marcos. There was no smile for him.

Marcos grinned back at her. "We were getting a little worried about you, kiddo. I thought maybe there was a problem with the flight."

"No, it was great."

Maggie reached out and squeezed her hand, pulling Sophia next to her. "We're so happy you decided to come in person."

"I wouldn't miss it for the world." Sophia's smile faded as her glance skipped past Lucas.

He got her message, though. She wouldn't miss Marcos and Maggie's wedding, even if it meant facing him again.

And yet he'd been standing here aching to

see her, the sensation so strong that he could barely talk.

Because you love her, you idiot. And you threw away your one chance to be with her.

He loved her.

Seeing her in the flesh made him realize just how much. She was selfless and compassionate, kind and sexy. And she really did take his damn breath away.

Forcing his voice from his chest took a super-human effort. "Good to see you, Sophia. I see the dry cleaner called you."

"That's right," Maggie said. "Lucas told us about what happened."

"Yes. It was quite an… Quite an experience," Sophia murmured.

Even from a couple of yards away he could see the hot color that stained her cheeks.

The minister cleared his throat. "If we're ready, could everyone stand on the little yellow marks? I have another wedding in a half-hour."

They all shuffled into position forming an inti-mate little U, which unfortunately put Lucas di-rectly across from Sophia.

No one had answered the obvious question that pulsed through his skull: how had Sophia gotten here? And why? He would have thought the last thing she'd want to do was face him after what he'd done.

Marcos reached out to clasp Maggie's hand, lifting it to his lips while Sophia smiled at the couple.

The orphanage had dubbed Lucas, Marcos and Sophia the Dynamic Trio.

It looked like his spot was no longer vacant. They now had Maggie to round out their little group.

Never in his life had Lucas felt so alone. So detached from everything he wanted out of life.

Maybe that's what refusing to put down roots did to you. Kept you from ever experiencing the true joy and pain of life. Yes, he'd avoided being hurt…avoided having those roots ripped up and his life torn apart. But at what cost? Those things were part of what made human beings who they were—times of pain making moments of joy that much sweeter.

As he gazed at Sophia, her image blurred suddenly and was replaced by that of a dark-haired girl with wide, trusting eyes. He peered deep inside his mind and tried to focus on the picture forming there.

Yes. He could see her. Her smile. Her laughter. Her tears.

When he came back to the present, she was still there. The same eyes. Same smile. He gulped. He'd seen those same tears.

He *knew* her. Had known her all his life. He'd just pushed away the memories, too afraid to walk down that road to the past.

And if he didn't tell her before she walked out of this chapel, he'd regret it for the rest of his life.

The short ceremony was a combination of tacky and charming, the way only Vegas weddings could be. But through it all Marcos's love for Maggie shone through.

And Lucas was more and more certain of his own love for Sophia.

Each time their eyes met, he wanted to stop the minister and tell her how sorry he was for leaving like he had. Tell her she'd been right about Marcos, about his ties with Brazil...about everything. He wanted to demand that she tell him if there was any chance for them. For him. Even though he had no idea what kind of life he could offer her.

The bride and groom's final kiss went on and on. When he glanced at Sophia, her head was down, and she stared at her toes, which he just noticed were housed in the same sexy shoes she'd been wearing the day they'd gone to the rental store. He was actually surprised she hadn't just shredded the dress or left it at the cleaners. But she hadn't. She'd worn it to the ceremony. That should tell him something, shouldn't it?

Marcos and Maggie finally parted, and from somewhere a shower of rice came down, hitting his skin with bitter little stings that seemed to taunt him.

Maggie laughed, blowing a kiss to Sophia. "Thank you so much for celebrating with us! We'll see you some time next week in Brazil."

Next week.

The realization came to him. This was it. The last time he would ever see Sophia, unless he did something about it.

Marcos grabbed his new bride's hand then paused beside him, murmuring in low tones. "You once gave me some very good advice about not being able to control everything in life. That if I loved Maggie, I should go after her. You were right." He slung an arm around her waist. "I'm handing back your own advice. If you care about her, don't let her walk away."

He then stepped back and slapped Lucas on the

back. "Don't be a stranger, bro. I expect to see a whole lot more of you in the future."

With that, the couple dashed out of the chapel to the limousine that was waiting to spirit them away.

He glanced across the carpet to see Sophia's eyes on him. She motioned down at the dress. "Thanks for having it cleaned."

"You're welcome."

The minister opened his arms as if pronouncing a final blessing and hinting that they should be on their way. "Thank you for being a part of today's ceremony. We wish you and yours a very happy evening."

Sophia took a step back. Then another. She was leaving. Right now.

He cleared his throat as she started to turn away. "Wait."

Glancing at the minister, he said, "Could you give us a minute?"

"A…minute?" Understanding dawned on his face, and he gave Lucas a knowing smile. "Of course. We still have a few moments before our next lucky couple arrives."

The man pressed something into his palm and

when Lucas turned it over he saw it was a business card. "Call us when you're ready."

He had no idea if Sophia would even accept his apology, much less agree to marry him.

But he wanted her to do both. More than anything.

The minister withdrew, leaving him alone with her. Taking a couple of steps forward, he hoped she could see the sincerity in his eyes. "I'm sorry for taking off like I did. It was wrong."

Sophia blinked at him. "I'm sorry I got emotional after...everything that happened."

"I thought I'd hurt you."

"You didn't at that moment. But I was afraid you would." She shrugged. "And you did."

The shot hit its mark and burrowed deep.

"Hell, Soph. I'm sorry. I've never been good at settling down in one place, and I..." He took a deep breath. "I don't know *how* to stick around. But I do know I love you, and I want to be with you. I want to go back to Brazil. With you, if you'll have me."

"You love me?"

He stepped even closer and touched his fingers to her cheek.

"I do. I saw you, Sophia. I finally remembered

what you looked like as a little girl. You were beautiful. I knew you would be. Just like that child in Dr. Figuereiro's office." He shook his head. "It's taken me thirty years to be able to look back and accept being a poor, filthy kid from a *favela*. But I can see it clearly now."

His fingertips brushed down her jaw until he cupped her chin. "I'm thinking about taking Dr. Figuereiro up on his offer. But only if you think you could fall in love with me someday."

"Someday? It's too late for that, Lucas."

A flash of hurt went through him, its bite worse—much worse—than the shower of rice a few minutes ago. He swallowed. "Well, then, I guess this is—"

"*Deus.* You're so quick to leap to the worst possible conclusion. It's too late because I'm *already* in love with you. I came to the United States to demand an explanation. And to tell you the truth about how I feel."

He hardly dared believe...

"Are you sure?"

"Absolutely."

He pressed a fist against his forehead and held it there as he tried to press back the volatile emotions that were beating against his eyelids, streaming through his veins. When he finally drew a deep breath, he looked up at her. "Don't go anywhere."

"I'm right here." She smiled, using the same words he'd used on their last night together. The relief and love he saw reflected on her face slid through him with a warmth that reached all the way down to his bones. A sense of certainty filled him as he drew her close—bent to kiss her. It was finally safe to put down those roots. Because Sophia would be right there beside him, her already deep system of roots providing an anchor for his, giving him a sense of something he'd been searching for his whole life: a place to call his own.

Home.

EPILOGUE

MARCOS GRABBED SOPHIA and swung her around the reception area of the empty clinic.

"Hey! What's the big idea?"

"I would tell you, but I promised Maggie I'd let her break the news. She's due here any minute."

Her brows went up. "News. What news?"

Lucas strolled out of the back, took one look at his brother's arm and gave a fair imitation of a disapproving scowl. "I'm willing to share most things, but my wife is not one of them."

Sophia brushed Marcos's fingers from her waist and crossed over to her husband of three weeks. "You don't have to share. I'm all yours. Besides, he says Maggie has…*news*."

Draping an arm over her shoulders, he drew her close. "*News*, huh? Very mysterious."

"Isn't it, though?" She batted her eyes at him.

Marcos glared at them as if they were spouting gibberish. "What's with you two?"

"Nothing," they said at the same time, then laughed.

After a whirlwind engagement, Lucas was settling into life at the clinic with an ease that surprised her. Dr. Figuereiro was still there and would be until Lucas finished all his certifications and licensing issues. They were looking at a year or a year and a half before everything could be legally handed off. But Lucas said he was fine with it. And Sophia was fine with accompanying him on volunteer trips to wherever his heart desired. There was no fear that he was suddenly going to get itchy feet and leave her, because she'd already told him she was sticking to him like glue. Her home was where he was.

The door opened, and the woman in question strolled in, holding something behind her back. She reached up to give Marcos a quick kiss on the mouth, and then looked up at him with narrowed eyes. "You told them, didn't you?"

"No, I…" He glanced at them. "Tell her I didn't say a word."

Sophia grinned. "He didn't. Really, he didn't."

"Okay, good, because I have something to show you."

She pulled her hand from behind her back and

wiggled a sheet of paper. Sophia took it and stared at it for a second before the tiny image took shape.

"You're pregnant?"

She hooked her arms around Marcos's waist. "Yes, we are. Six weeks, to be exact."

"What the hell? They scooped us." The statement burst from Lucas, and it set off a fit of giggles that Sophia couldn't contain. The giggle turned into a laugh that swelled and grew until she couldn't breathe, couldn't talk, tears streaming down her face.

She finally gulped back the sound. "Sorry about that. Congratulations!" Another choked laugh emerged at the end of the sentence.

Maggie's brows drew together in a frown, while Marcos's mouth opened and closed like a landed fish. Maggie huffed out a breath. "Is this a Brazilian thing, because I don't see what's so funny?"

Biting her lip hard, Sophia finally got herself under control. Then she reached over and squeezed Lucas's hand. "Show them."

Shaking his head and still muttering to himself, he went behind the reception desk and retrieved his own piece of paper and came around to the other side.

He handed it to his brother, who stared down at the sheet. "You…you…?"

Maggie evidently realized what had happened, because she shook a finger at them before coming over and catching Sophia up in a quick hug. "You guys! You too?"

"Yes. Eight weeks. Why do you think we were in such a hurry to get married?"

They'd invited Sophia's parents to the simple ceremony—something that had taken some doing, since Lucas hadn't wanted them anywhere near her. Although there were still some old wounds that needed to heal, her folks had done what they felt best all those years ago—leaving her where she could get the government-funded care they couldn't afford. They'd hoped she'd be adopted and given a better life than what they could provide. That hadn't happened, and as time passed, they'd been too ashamed to ask the orphanage to return her to their care.

Lucas held a hand out to his brother, and Marcos grabbed it, pulling him into a tight embrace.

"Congratulations, bro."

"You too. We seem to be following in each other's footsteps."

It wasn't just marriage and the pregnancy they

had in common. Lucas had joined his brother in providing free health care in the *favela* where they'd been born. They hoped to expand from one day a week to two days over the next year, recruiting more doctors to join in the effort.

"We do seem to be, don't we?" Marcos paused for a second before continuing. "Maybe it's not each other's footsteps we're following. Maybe it's the path Dad laid down for us. He was determined to give us a better life. And he did. Even if he never had a chance to witness it."

Lucas glanced at where their wives were exchanging plans for the future, and thought about the unlikely way he and his brother had found exactly what they were looking for. "You know, I wouldn't be so sure about Dad not witnessing it. I think he might just know."

* * * * *